Praise for *What Goes Around*
A novel of power, love and war

"...story is compelling... Vietnam flashbacks are very accurate."
Dave "Doc" Kirby, *Book Bits*

"...retrospective narrative, colorful dialogue and skillfully crafted characters..."
Aleta Boudreaux, author of *Song of the White Swan*

"...fast-paced, tough and causal...hard to put down...long rambling, artistic descriptions simply don't exist...something important is always about to happen...a roller-coaster ride that doesn't stop until the book is finished...powerful, tightly written and entertaining...the class of a serious novel."
Jeremy Brown, author of *The Serpent and the Staff*

"I could not put it down...a fast paced thriller and a critical look at failed human systems."
Julius Brandstatter, Ph.D., San Francisco State University

"...an excellent read...tight without wasting words."
Ciara Luvstar, author of *Faces*

"...one of the most enjoyable paperbacks to be published in some time... the scenes, the setting and the dialog keep you immersed in the story from beginning to end"
Darrell Bain, Author of *Medics Wild*

PACIFIC COAST PRESS publications
By David O'Neal

What Goes Around
The Pact With Bruno
Choosing To Kill (1999)

The Pact With Bruno

The Pact With Bruno

David O'Neal

David O'Neal

A Pacific Coast Press publication

The Pact With Bruno
A Pacific Coast Press publication, October 1998

ISBN 0-9660851-1-6

First Edition

Pacific Coast Press, PO Box 26857, San Jose, CA 95159
Visit our web site at http://www.pacificcoastpress.com

To the readers who have found something special
in Doug Carlson. Your interest in him is a source
of tremendous support. Thank you
for sharing my dream.

Jerry's concern shifted to pride. He recalled watching Doug's valiant display of grit and determination on that Vietnam battlefield where he completely disregarded his own safety in order to secure it for others.

Now, Doug displayed that same level of devotion for a lost love, one he was helpless to save at the time and was now fearful for a new love he might not be able to protect. He smiled, savoring the wonderfully painful dilemmas of the heart in the uncharted matters of love.

The Pact With Bruno, Chapter Fourteen

Chapter One

The chauffeur opened the passenger door of the white limousine. A freshly scented woman's foot stretched to touch the sculpted walkway. The evening air had begun to cool. The slit of her full-length, black silk gown exposed her right leg to mid-thigh.

The other foot followed gracefully as she rose from the lush interior of the new luxury vehicle.

A man dressed in a black tuxedo with a red silk bow tie and matching cumberbun slid across the soft leather seat to exit behind her. As he stepped away from the vehicle, their chauffeur smartly closed the door. Positioning himself at the wheel, he pulled the vehicle forward and parked it in the waiting garage.

The couple took several steps toward the gaily-decorated, brightly-lit entrance of mama's home then paused to see who was arriving in the following limo.

Sammy's striking blonde beauty was enviable. She beamed upon recognizing Kely's face through the window of the limo that was just pulling up.

The chauffeur rushed to hold the door.

Turning, Kely placed both of her feet on the walkway before she stood. The two unusually attractive women greeted each other with a fond embrace. Smooth powdered cheeks touched in the waning sunlight. Lightly their kisses brushed each other's ear.

Kely's short darker hair contrasted well with Sammy's much longer locks.

As the women stepped away from the door of the limo, Jerry emerged and shifted toward Doug. The two men moved closer and shook hands, greeting each other with their usual male ritual. Each woman turned to greet the other's man with an embrace and a soft kiss.

While Kely's lips brushed Doug's, painful memories from nine months earlier flooded his heart. Last December he could not have imagined any of the life changes he now accepted as being commonplace.

His six-foot frame, sandy-colored hair and firm tanned body made him look like a professional surfer, but his job as an investment manager was in a very different league.

Each woman placed a gloved hand around the arm of her escort. They moved forward without speaking.

A chill in the air became apparent as an evening breeze caressed bare skin. Sammy squeezed Doug's arm and snuggled closer for the added warmth it offered.

Another limousine pulled forward as the last one moved toward the garage parking area.

On the other side of the portico, two uniformed servants opened the front doors of Bruno's mansion, stepped aside and bowed at the waist. The couples moved into the subtly designed tile, mahogany and rosewood foyer to join other guests already waiting in a long receiving line.

The line reached fifteen feet ahead where mama sat.

Tonight was her birthday. Her eighty-nine years of friendships, entwined with near forgotten memories, would fill spacious rooms with laughter that evening.

Sammy chatted with the woman standing in line ahead of her. Soon Kely joined them in conversation. Soft chamber music played in the distance. Waves of merriment washed pleasantly in and out of the background.

Other guests arrived and waited in line behind them.

Jerry's slim six-foot frame stepped aside searching the faces ahead for his grandmother. Finally sitting at the head of the line, a few feet through the main door, mama caught his inquiring glance. She smiled warmly and waved before returning to her guests.

He ran his hand across shiny black hair to assure it was still brushed straight back. Feeling confident that it was, he stepped closer to his companions.

Recollections occupied Doug as he stood silently in line next to Sammy and Kely.

For a moment the battles with Mr. C and his goons played savagely in Doug's mind. His festive mood quickly dwindled. The death of Catherine brought him the most pain and that first meeting with Bruno still haunted him. Then he had fought several bloody battles with the mob, but now he worked for Bruno Sebastino, the Godfather of the Los Angeles Mafia. Often he wondered about the rhyme and reason behind the hand that fate had dealt him.

He remembered the attack on him and Catherine at the hospital by several of Mr. C's goons and how the feds were readily available to help them. Otherwise it would have been fatal to them both. But, then rather than giving up Bruno to the feds, as he would normally have done, fate twisted his life so that he went to work for him.

Bruno had not been a part of the war with Mr. C. He had dealt fairly and honorably with Doug and owed him the debt of saving Jerry's life. While Doug was long over the initial discomfort, he still found himself with lingering doubts about his decision to stay involved.

Federal Agent Townsen and his men had assisted him and yet he willingly turned his back on them. If the forces of karma did exist in the universe, then its twists and turns were certainly affecting Doug.

A blast of excitement made him aware of the moment. Standing two couples in line behind them, Jerry recognized his cousin, Luigi, Clarice's only son, and his third wife, Brandy, a former casino dealer and most recently a starring Vegas show girl.

Luigi's pudgy appearance and his array of fine clothes contrasted greatly with Brandy's svelte looks and gaudy party clothes. They both smiled as if to say they were already having a grand time.

Jerry's excitement controlled him. "Hey, long time no see, cuz. Where you been keeping yourself?" Jerry moved toward him with outstretched arms.

The two men shared a quick family embrace. Luigi kissed him excitedly on the cheek.

Quizzing his cousin through a growing animation, Jerry asked. "How's things going at the *GP*?"

Looking confused, Doug turned to Sammy and whispered. "What's *GP* stand for?"

"That's what everybody at the casino in Las Vegas calls *The Golden Phoenix*." He nodded and watched as Luigi introduced Jerry to his wife. The couples all shifted forward in the line.

Jerry turned to his party and chattered through his elation. "This is my cousin, Luigi, from Las Vegas." Doug extended a hand as Jerry made the introductions. Kely stepped forward and Jerry introduced them.

Luigi spoke to her. "You're looking especially beautiful tonight, Ms. Walker." Kely smiled and stepped back knowing that Luigi considered himself to be quite an accomplished ladies man.

Abandoning Brandy behind him, Luigi stepped toward Sammy with an exaggerated smile.

She extended her hand.

His devouring eyes met hers. His smile expanded to cover his entire face.

"Hi there, Sammy, nice to see you again. You're quite a knock-out this evening, as usual."

He bowed then kissed the back of her hand.

Surprised, she withdrew it and wiped it discreetly on the back of her dress.

"Hey, what about me, Louie?" Brandy stepped forward and gave Luigi a jealous pinch on his elbow.

Instantly, he turned his attention back to her with an exaggerated apology for having walked away.

Jerry's eyes sparkled mischievously. He turned to face Doug. With inquiring eyes Doug looked to Sammy. Kely giggled. Sammy made a sly gag-me face then she and Kely turned toward the front of the line.

Sporting a conniving smile, Jerry moved a little closer to Doug explaining in a whisper his cousin's fascination with casino women and especially with the very beautiful ones like Sammy.

An elderly couple finished reminiscing of their childhood with mama during the early part of the century and moved forward into the reception area.

The line inched forward.

Bruno approached mama and she beamed. To many people his stout frame made him appear like a giant, but his gentle demeanor made him more approachable.

He kissed his mother on the top of her gray head. Mama raised her hand and placed frail fingers on his bulky arm. She kissed his neck and spoke soft, loving words into the ear of her only son.

The years had been very good for the both of them.

Bruno's first few jobs for the mob kept him away from most of the violence occurring in the Bronx. In those early days mama pleaded that he learn to use his mind rather than his muscle. Later he grew into a big man, but his wit had become the stronger.

His growing reputation as a smooth talker and consummate peacemaker were hard earned during years of intervention in Mafia problems and was well deserved. Power, respect and lots of money had been his reward and no one questioned that he had rightfully earned them all.

Doug's somber mood shifted upon noticing that both Sammy and Kely now stared at him as they chatted.

He smiled, shielding a flash of discomfort. Their warm smiles of approval surrounded him.

He relaxed a bit more.

Slowly Doug's upset about the past subsided and his contemplation turned to Sammy, a beautiful, educated and independent-minded woman who now worked as a black-jack dealer in *The Golden Phoenix*, a mob-owned and operated Las Vegas casino.

Her striking beauty earned her outrageous tips. Her dealer skills earned Bruno's casino millions of dollars.

Hitching a ride on the casino's corporate jet, she commuted to Los Angeles every Friday afternoon to be with Doug and then returned each Monday morning for her job. Reluctant at first, she chose to date him only after repeated assurances from both Bruno and Jerry that he was not involved in any of the mob's nefarious business.

Another of mama's childhood friends shook hands with Bruno, chatted briefly and exited toward the reception.

Kely and Jerry were next in line.

They stepped forward.

Jerry whispered to Doug. "You okay, pal?"

"Yeah, I'm fine." Uncomfortably he looked away before continuing his response. "Just remembering some of those things that happened to me last year."

"Well, cut that out! Can we have only laughter and smiles from you tonight?"

Taking a deep breath Doug promised. "That should be no problem." He smiled uneasily and turned to face Sammy. After catching her eye she moved closer. Her hand sought, found his and then softly enclosed it.

The next couple moved away from mama.

Kely stepped closer, leaned down and reached to hug her. They held the embrace as each woman spoke treasured loving words to the other.

With quick mutual kisses they parted.

With a snappy graceful move Jerry took her place.

"Gramma, you're looking wonderful." They hugged a few seconds, ended with a quick kiss then he stood.

Stepping to the right, he grabbed Bruno's extended hand. Mama's eyes followed him.

"Papa, how have you been?" Bruno's hands encircled Jerry's. The handshake slowly changed into a deep bear hug. Father and son shared each other's warmth.

Mama's tired eyes lingered and drank the shared love her men demonstrated for one another.

Sammy stepped close and mama spoke. "Child, how long has it been since you last visited with me?"

"Much too long, Mama." Sammy leaned to offer a hug. Their cheeks touched for a heartbeat. Sammy stood and her smile reflected her feelings of pleasure.

Mama's eyes turned toward Doug. In this light her aged skin appeared softer. Her warm heart and many years of life offered much to those she loved.

He stepped forward to face her.

"And you, young man. Has my son kept you too busy to visit a lonely old woman who might pass-on any day?" She smiled as her warm hands reached for him.

"No, Mama, I'm sorry for not visiting more often, but that's not the case at all." Doug leaned closer to offer her a peck on the cheek. He felt the heat of growing embarrassment from such an innocent act.

Her arms reached to enclose him. "Well, I expect to see you and this beautiful child here more often."

Doug nodded and stood.

Mama reached again for Sammy's hand. They clasped fingers. Mama felt Sammy's rings and asked. "Are you two planning a wedding yet?"

Through a blush Sammy responded. "No, Mama. It's still too early for us to think about that."

From three feet away Bruno's voice boomed. "Nonsense. If Jerry and Kely are considering it, then the two of you can certainly do the same." His massive body nodded a silent approval of his comment.

Sammy replied. "We promise you'll both be among the first to know about our special day when it's time."

Another couple inched forward behind them.

Doug extended a hand to Bruno and stepped toward him as he spoke. "This is quite an elegant affair you've arranged. Thanks for sending the limo to pick us up."

"My boy, I'll always do for you exactly what I'd do for Jerry." Bruno took Doug's hand as he had done with his own son, then followed it with an all-enclosing bear hug.

Doug enjoyed the warmth, but felt some discomfort, not from the hug but from his business dealings with Bruno and of course his informal position with the mob.

His mind wandered onto that first business meeting with Bruno. He had tried to keep their dealings limited to social ones, but Bruno insisted that Doug's years of banker experience could be of good use to each of them.

With every objection he expressed, Bruno was willing to compromise almost anything to accommodate his wishes. Eventually Doug had carved a unique relationship with one of the most powerful underworld figures on the entire West Coast.

While he was not interested in being involved with any

of the mob's illegal activities or in handling any of their
ill-gotten gains, he had offered to control, manage and invest Bruno's clean money and that would become the
backbone of their business relationship.

As the hug ended, Doug's mind released the memories.
Sammy moved to him and found his hand again.

Bruno shook his head. "You two are so perfect for
each other. Is there a problem, Sammy?"

Grabbing Bruno's forearm as they walked, she responded with a smile. "No, but we'll make those plans
when the time is finally right for us. You know that all of
your coaxing will have little effect."

They chuckled.

Bruno joked with them as they walked to the reception
area. "Don't wait too long, son. I've seen how other men
look at this beauty in the casino."

📖

Otis Townsen stood in front of a heavily armed selec-
tion of his best agents. Their discussion of the past hour
outlined their participation in a raid on a local Mafia
nightclub that was scheduled for later in the evening.

Dressed in green battle fatigues, combat boots, body
armor, web belts and side arms, the energy of the highly
trained agents was electric. Several sported automatic rifles with laser sights. Dark green Kevlar helmets rested on
the floor at their feet.

Now they waited for the arrival of a joint task force
from the Los Angeles Police Department. Since their undercover intelligence formed the basis for the FBI opera-

tion, they would be included in the raid only as a matter of professional courtesy.

Although Townsen did not trust the messenger, his own investigation of the lead appeared to substantiate it.

His red hair and lighter complexion spoke volumes about his Irish heritage. Combined with his firm business-like demeanor, the combination was hard to forget.

Six men in black camouflaged fatigues wearing black and green face paint burst through the rear doors of the briefing room. Everyone turned to look.

Detective Jason Harris followed them, but he wore his usual dark business suit. The LA swat team members took empty seats near the rear of the room.

There were somber faces and strong rigid bodies.

Once seated there was silence.

Harris continued walking to the front of the room.

He offered an open hand to Townsen. "At last we finally have the chance to meet. I'm Detective Harris, LAPD." His beefy hand was strong. Years of inadequate activity had laid waste to a much more powerful body.

Extending a hand, the tall red-haired man responded firmly. "It's a pleasure to meet you. I'm Agent Otis Townsen, FBI Special Operations Division."

"Have you briefed your men yet?" Harris asked.

"Yes, I've presented everything except the club's name as you requested. We've also reviewed your map of the club and the photos of the targeted suspects."

"That just about covers the preliminaries." Motioning as though he might take control, Harris asked. "Do you mind if I speak to your men?"

"No, not at all." Townsen stepped back and leaned on

the edge of a nearby table.

"Gentlemen, our target this evening is called *The Neon Phoenix*. It's the pride of the Mafia and of Bruno Sebastino, who is widely believed to be the Los Angeles Godfather. There's a very good chance that he'll be there tonight. As a result, I expect it to be heavily guarded by some very bad dudes. So, gentlemen, do not relax your guard this evening for even a second."

A young member of the swat team raised his hand.

Harris paused and pointed to him.

"Begging your pardon, sir, but my woman and I do a considerable amount of clubbing and I've never heard of a club with that particular name."

"That's right, Reynolds, and if you had, you'd be in very deep-shit with me because it's an exclusive, members-only club run by the LA Mafia. It's only open to their most trusted members and their families."

The man wisecracked through a big grin. "Well, that certainly explains it." Several of his buddies laughed.

Harris glared at them.

There was instant silence.

He continued. "Gentlemen, this will not be a cakewalk so get that idea out of your head. Mr. Sebastino takes everything about his business very seriously and you'll know exactly why when you've completed this operation."

Townsen stood and addressed Harris. "Have you worked out the deployments?"

Harris reached into a pocket for notes and then stopped in mid-movement to glare at Townsen as though he was standing too close to him.

The two men stared for an instance. Townsen relented

and sat back on the edge of the table.

"Yes, we'll cover that now." Harris said.

📖

Party guests crowded the lavishly decorated veranda:
mama's friends and family, Bruno's associates and close
friends, local politicians, trusted reporters and the creme
de la creme of the West Coast Mafia establishment. They
clustered in small comfortable groups. Standing on the
edge of the veranda near the stairs to a lower deck, Jerry
and Doug chatted and stayed close to their ladies.

Kely giggled with delight as she watched Sammy
grimace after taking a sip of Doug's drink.

Recovering, Sammy forced a smile. "I've never been
able to handle coffee-flavored drinks. No matter what's
added to them, they taste so yuckie."

Jerry commented. "How can a classy dame like you not
survive on coffee or at least like it a little? In your line of
work I'd expect you to drink it by the gallon."

He smiled.

"Well, Jerry, you're just full of insignificant tidbits of
wisdom about the working women of Las Vegas or is this
just one more piece of chauvinist male myth?" Sammy retorted, hand on hip.

Gleefully Kely cheered. "Give it to him, girl."

Doug smiled at Sammy, knowing she was extremely
capable of dishing it out. He picked up his drink from the
delicately carved railing and took a sip.

His fingers toyed briefly with a paper decoration.

Jerry wailed. "Hey, whose side are you on?"

"This is the year for supporting our sisters, so I guess you lose, honey." Kely smiled at him, sent an air-kiss and moved closer.

Turning to Doug he sought comfort. "Well, I suppose us guys will have to stick together then."

Doug obliged him. "Semper Fi, buddy."

They bumped fists as their usual salute of unity.

Playfully Sammy continued. "You guys aren't going to get started on that Marine stuff…?"

A booming, cultured voice interrupted her. "Ladies and gentlemen, may I have your attention? Dinner is now being served in the main ballroom."

📖

The rear doors of the first swat vehicle burst open.

The clash of metal on metal shattered the still night air. Harris' team poured-out wearing their full battle gear. The sound of heavy boots produced a troubled cadence that tolled of impending violence.

Thirty feet away the two squads of federal agents carried out the same movements from similar armored vehicles. As the last man cleared the open doors, someone on the inside pulled them shut and the vehicles sped off to a nearby staging area.

The men ran for cover in an abandoned building where they regrouped into their original teams. Each man's helmet contained a transceiver with earphones and a boom mike for maintaining verbal contact among themselves and with Townsen, their command leader. Harris remained in one of the swat vehicles to monitor radio transmissions and to coordinate their activities.

Townsen gave the final orders. "Team A, advance under cover and secure the rear entrances."

"Roger." Four officers responded and immediately exited at a double-time pace in that direction.

"Team B, move to the roof, cover all escape routes and detain everyone you encounter. There will be absolutely no exceptions!"

"Yes, sir." The four officers responded, then proceeded aggressively to their posts.

"Team C, you will accompany me through a locked, and hopefully, unused side door. We will secure four primary positions inside the building. At this point stealth is of the utmost importance. Use your dart pistols to subdue all resistance you encounter before the mission is ready to be launched. Any questions?"

A number of the anxious men responded. "No, sir."

"Then take your positions."

"Yes, sir." The eight remaining men responded and began moving to their posts.

Townsen moved forward with them as he spoke to the command vehicle. "Harris, what's the status of the uniforms that you've included?"

"Nine by four are waiting at three miles. We'll move on this side with your command."

Townsen replied. "Roger. Team A, report."

After a brief pause the response came from its team leader. "Team A in position, sir. Ready in two."

"Team B, report."

"Team B still in transit, sir."

As Townsen's team arrived at the unused door, an

agent ran forward with a large leather bag of tools. An industrial bolt cutter was selected. Within seconds the door was open and agents poured into the dark corridor.

Narrow beams of light penetrated the darkness from many different angles.

They moved in three directions to secure their posts.

Townsen remained near the door. He drew his automatic pistol and activated the slide, placing a live round into the chamber.

His earphone sprang to life. "Sir, Team B is in position and ready to move."

"Sir, Team A in position and ready."

Lingering in the darkness, Townsen spoke. "Team C, report when all stations are secure."

His heart felt the excitement. He knew it raced at the possibilities. Finally he was in a position to capture Bruno Sebastino and hopefully a lot of his top-level associates.

What if Bruno isn't here?

Briefly he conjectured whether any of Bruno's men could ever be persuaded to give up *The Don*. Probably not, but at least he hoped it would happen.

Another report broke the silence. "Sir, Team C, station 2 in position and ready to go on your command."

Townsen waited.

His thoughts jumped to Doug Carlson. He was still disappointed that Carlson had not offered him more info last year when he had fought Mr. C's men. He was certain that Bruno and his organization would have been the next ones to go down, but suddenly Doug's war with the mob ended without any further explanation.

"Sir, Team C, station 1 in position and ready. One intruder neutralized. Situation under control."

The last two teams reported to him and Townsen relayed it to Harris. "Control, all positions secured. Ready for uniforms to move."

Excitedly, Harris responded. "Insiders, move in two minutes. Uniforms, we have a go. Move it, now!"

Chapter Two

The first two courses of mama's birthday dinner had been served quietly. Fifty-eight places were arranged in the spacious ballroom with eleven servants tending the dinner needs of the guests.

Dottie, mama's social secretary, worked until the very last minute assigning the guest seats around the table. Her graying hair always arranged in a bun on top of her head made her look like most people's recollections of their second grade school teacher.

Expanding one's personal horizons and social interaction skills through polite conversation with strangers was a high priority for mama. One could count on her social affairs to be the fullest expression of that time-honored, elegant philosophy.

The third course began arriving.

Bruno tapped the rim of his crystal with a spoon. All

eyes focused toward him. The conversation stopped.

He stood to make a toast.

"Ladies and gentlemen. Thank you for your attendance in our home this evening. We gather tonight to praise a woman of great stature, to celebrate her many years of undying devotion to family and friends and to share the healthful attainment of her eighty-nine years. This woman has been a rock in the community. For many of her years she has been the strength that guided me and steadfastly nurtured her growing family.

"At various times she has been my teacher, my confidant and often my best friend. While I sometimes tried not to take her advice, I usually did so. This woman who is quite special to many of you is also very special to me. I would like to offer a toast of love, good health and continued long life to my mother." He paused.

"Ladies and gentlemen raise your glasses for a salute to Maria Rosalie Ricadonna Sebastino, My mama."

Many at the large table stood.

Mama picked up her flute and leaned back in her overly soft chair. With glasses held high numerous chants of *Hear-Hear*, *Happy Birthday* and *Long life to you, Mama* filled the hall.

The servants paused during the toast, smiled warmly toward mama and many offered her a single nod.

She beamed with pleasure.

After several seconds the next course was being enjoyed by all around the table.

Quietly Bruno moved toward mama.

She held out a feeble hand. He kissed it and spoke to her in a soft voice. He helped her to stand then returned to his seat. Silence covered the room as mama began speaking in an aged, broken voice.

"My very dear friends, I thank you for sharing this special evening of celebration with my family, friends and me. Your friendships, mutual love and support during the past half-century, and more, are the jewels of life I cherish. My heart is full. I offer thanks for it all."

She reached for her champagne and raised it.

"To my son and daughter who have both added so much to my life. I raise my glass to praise you."

The rest of the room followed mama's lead.

"Bruno, Clarice, I love you both with all my heart."

She raised her glass higher.

Her gaze moved back and forth between her two treasures. The room erupted to seal the toast.

Clarice moved toward her mother.

Jerry stood to make the next toast.

An elegantly dressed butler entered the room, paused then moved directly behind Bruno's chair before stopping. He leaned forward and whispered.

"Excuse me, sir. There is an urgent phone call for you from a gentleman named Detective Harris. He apologizes for interrupting your festive dinner, but says that he has important matters to discuss with you."

"Thank you, Carlos."

Bruno exited to a nearby room and picked up the waiting telephone receiver. "Hello, Detective Harris. How can I be of help to you this evening?"

"Well, sir. I apologize for bringing you bad news on such a happy occasion, but your nightclub on Carmel Street was raided this evening by the feds. Most of the staff were arrested and one of your close friends, a Mr. Gilberto Leone, is among them."

"Do you know what prompted this event?"

"No. I was very surprised yesterday when the feds called me asking for local officers to join with their task force. I sent a team, but only did so reluctantly."

"Do you know what they were looking for?"

"Not really, sir, but there was some talk about you actually being on the premises. I suspect that they were looking to arrest you, too. I'm at the club now. Is there anything I can do to assist you while I'm still here?"

Bruno paused.

"Can you get Mr. Leone out of there and away from the feds without causing too much trouble?"

"I'm not exactly sure, but I'll give it a shot. The federal agent who is running the show is a real hard-ass. On second thought, Mr. Sebastino, I'll pull out all the stops for you on this. One way or another I'll get your friend released to my custody. I'll take him to the West LA Station if that's convenient."

"Good. I'll be there to pick him up from you within the hour." Bruno paused then continued. "Detective Harris, why didn't you call me about this yesterday?"

"I'm sorry, sir. I would have been glad to do that, but I didn't actually know the location of the raid until it was disclosed by the feds this evening."

"Oh."

In the past, reports to Bruno about Detective Harris were conflicting and this conversation with him failed to clear up his growing confusion about the man.

"Thank you for working with me." Harris added.

"Sure." Bruno hung up the phone, returned to the dining room and scanned the faces of his guests.

The toasts were done and plates were being cleared for the arrival of Mama's birthday cake. Bruno moved toward his friend and personal attorney, Jacob Feldman.

"Jay, Bert was arrested a little while ago by the feds at *The Neon Phoenix*. A local badge is moving him to the West LA station for us to pick him up."

"Is there time for cake before we go?" Jay asked.

"Of course."

📖

Harris pointed his finger. "I'm taking that clown down to the precinct. He's a major player behind a lot of the local shit, so I want to get a big piece of him." Detective Harris turned away from Townsen.

"So get your butt moving!"

The man's eyes swelled in surprise.

His fine tailored suit, clean arrest record and life-long connections to Bruno were of no value to him now. Two of Harris' black-clad agents grabbed his arms and escorted him roughly toward the main door.

"Detective Harris, what do you think you're doing?" Townsen felt his temperature rise.

"I'm taking this punk in for a few more questions."

"That's no street punk. He's just an administrative flunky for the club. Who you trying to shit?"

"Back off, Mister! Did you forget this is my show?"

"So why the sudden change of plans?"

"That's classified." Harris barked.

"Shit. I should have known you'd eventually get on to pulling something reckless like this."

Townsen turned in disgust and walked away.

Harris moved toward the door where his men waited with Mr. Leone. As he approached they began walking toward the transport vehicle.

Harris reached into his pocket.

The chrome-plated .38 special was wrapped in a handkerchief and for the moment devoid of fingerprints. He stroked it with pleasure then withdrew his hand.

One of the officers stepped forward and unlocked the back door of Harris' car.

The other one directed Mr. Leone toward it.

"Hold it, Reynolds." Harris ordered.

"Sir?"

"I want you to shoot this scum-bag fucker. I want him dead and that's an order."

Reynolds drew his holstered weapon, but hesitated. A confused look covered his face. "Sir?"

"Now, god-damn it!"

Two semiautomatic pistol shots cracked in the night air. Reynolds turned away from the unprovoked killing to hide the grimace on his face.

Hearing footsteps in the distance Harris moved forward quickly placing the chrome pistol into Mr. Leone's limp hand. He stood to review the scene then leaned forward to adjust the man's arm.

Harris yelled toward the crowd gathering nearby. "Can we get a photographer over here!"

📖

As the limousine pulled away from the curb of the West LA precinct station, Bruno spoke in a soft tone. "Jay, this is just too hard to believe. I can't understand why Bert would do something so damn stupid."

"Me neither. He's about the last person I'd expect to try and pull anything as foolish as that."

Bruno shook his head and sighed. "That's not the Bert I knew." Confusion filled his voice. "A whole lifetime of being his friend and I never saw that side of him. It's just impossible, I tell you."

"Just remember only the good things about him now. Let this one foolish action be forgotten." Jay whispered. He was shocked too, but did not have all the childhood memories of Bert that Bruno did.

He offered a friendly pat on Bruno's knee.

Images of growing up in the Bronx and being children together flooded Bruno's stunned awareness.

He voiced his memories. "We did everything together as kids. We even served together in the Navy in the South Pacific during WW2. For god's sake, we were even the *best man* at each other's wedding. I just can't believe he's really gone." Repeatedly he shook his head.

Briefly he thought about Bert's wife.

"Jay, let's drive over to see Sara before it gets any later, so I can tell her in person what's happened. I don't want her to hear a single word of this from anyone else, especially the police."

After giving the limo driver Sara's address they sat in a gripping stunned silence.

Eventually Bruno spoke of Bert again. "He was very

wise with his money so I know Sara and the girls will be well cared for and never want for things. Jay, can you help her settle Bert's affairs?"

Jay nodded.

"You do whatever needs to be done and send me all of the bills. I want my childhood friend to have the best funeral possible. Damn, I just can't believe this is really happening." He shook his head.

Jay nodded again.

Bruno leaned his head on the back of the seat.

He closed his eyes to alternatively envision Bert's face as a man and then as a little boy. At 66 Bruno knew that both happiness and sadness were the necessary prizes of a long and healthy life.

📖

After midnight, the crowd at *The Watering Hole* usually dwindled to only a few of the heartiest drinkers. LAPD cops from tonight's raid had made it a full house. Even now, most were still there.

Drunken laughter masked feelings of relief that the raid had been so successful. The death of one civilian, though not pleasant to most, was an acceptable loss considering how bloody it might have been. Since no one else was injured, especially among the cops, their reasons for continued celebration were many.

In a corner booth away from most of the merriment sat three men with another agenda. Detective Harris had already been on the mob's payroll, but that had ended last year. Officer Reynolds' ambition had made him a killer in spite of his feelings, but he was willing to pursue his share of the mob's easy money. Officer Garcia's lifestyle had moved him far beyond his humble family roots. Now he needed more money and sadly when he drank he forgot about the teachings from his past.

Harris had pulled a lot of departmental strings and promised more than he could deliver to get them both temporarily assigned to the swat team during the raid.

Having far more than enough to drink Garcia shouted. "It still sounds much too risky to me."

"Keep your voice down." Harris warned.

He had spent too much time and effort to let his plan die before it was half done. "It's only risky if we somehow manage to fuck it up."

Reynolds nodded. "That may be right, but it has me a bit worried, too. There's always the chance that some more of this unexpected stuff will happen. Then what would we do?"

Harris lashed out at them. "You two are really a pair of limp-dick losers. What could possibly happen?"

"What if we get caught before your big plan swings into full action?" Reynolds asks.

Garcia nodded.

"How can we get caught if we kill them all? Who'll be left to snitch on us?" Harris waited for a response.

"That's not what I meant. What if someone sees us or somebody else snitches on us?" Reynolds clamored.

"There is no one else, just the three of us. It seems like the kind of safety you want is to kill everyone at the scene, right? I can live with that."

Harris looked to Garcia for his support.

From his somber mood Garcia did not offer any. Instead he asked. "Okay, but what if something else, unexpected happens?"

Reynolds added. "Like earlier tonight, when you decided to pop that guy. Excuse me, I mean when you decided that I was going to pop him. What if that kind of shit happens again? Doing all of this *by the seat of our pants* seems to be too risky to me."

"Is that what's got you so hot under the collar?" Harris shot back at him.

"For starters that's one."

"Well that little last minute change removed a lot of the guesswork for us when the next part of the job is finished." Harris smiled as if he had made a genius move with his modified plan.

"Your last minute changes are what's bugging me. It leaves too much for me to personally worry about."

Harris groaned. "Give me a break. The timing this evening was so perfect. I just couldn't pass it up."

Through a disbelieving look Reynolds questioned. "I'm not that dumb, am I?" He looked to Garcia who managed a bit of a frown and then shook his head. "You had that gun ready to drop on him so you must have planned it without bothering to tell either of us."

Shaking his head Harris barked. "Back-off, Reynolds. I'm not explaining my every move to you, rookie. Are you with us or not?"

Both Harris and Garcia stared at him.

Reynolds inhaled deeply and exhaled quickly as a signal of his growing resignation. "I am, but I still think this operation's going way too fast."

"Maybe, but that was always the plan, if you remember." Harris responded.

Garcia mumbled something and both men turned to face him. He repeated himself. "Too fast is right. It's going way too fast for me, too."

Harris rolled his eyes and relented. "Okay, that's it. You guys win. I'll mention it to Mr. Sebastino when we have our lunch meeting on Monday."

Both men's eyes grew big.

Garcia asked. "And when did you make that date?"

"Tonight. After his friend was shot I played heavily on his grief and made a few hints that maybe it could all have been avoided if I had been more involved."

Reynolds added. "You sneaky son-of-a-bitch, when did you plan on getting around to telling us about that?"

"I was getting to it earlier, but your whining about not following orders got in the way." Harris criticized.

"So does this mean that we don't have to move as fast as we had first thought?"

"That will depend on whether he gives me a job tomorrow or not." Harris bragged.

📖

Bruno and Jay had just left Bert's home. Sara's tears had subsided for the moment. The girls had been called and were on their way home to be with their mother.

Jay spoke to his dear friend. "This is a fairly tough life for men like you who also have a family. I don't think I could handle it, if you know what I mean."

"It does get to me sometimes, but just now and then.

When the kids were young I didn't think about it very much. Now with them all grown up and having a couple of grandkids I'm thinking more and more about it." Bruno confided to him.

"Does this mean you'll be retiring any time soon?"

Laughing, Bruno responded. "You're not the first one to mention that to me, but I'm feeling too young to look at it in any serious way. Maybe next year will find me liking it a little more."

Jay was two years older than Bruno. He whispered as if he could barely talk. "I've thought about that too. I would certainly enjoy spending more time with my grand-kids and living a longer life than my dear old mama did."

Chapter Three

Threads of silver light beamed through tiny openings in the closed curtains. Doug reached for the ringing phone on his nightstand. The clock radio indicated it was 7:59.

Next to him Sammy rolled over, covered her head with a fluffy pillow and tried to stay asleep.

He paused for a moment to collect his faded thoughts then answered the phone. "Hello."

"Hey, Doug. It was certainly great seeing the two of you last night." Bruno knew that no one would ever offer a single word of complaint about his calling them too early on a Sunday morning.

"Hi, Bruno. How are you doing this morning?" Doug closed his eyes and silently yawned.

Sammy stirred upon hearing Bruno's name mentioned and grabbed Doug's pillow for the extra sound protection.

He did not struggle with her to keep it.

Bruno's voice boomed in his ear. "I'm good, thank you. I'm feeling just fine. We're planning an afternoon barbecue at the house later today and I'd like for you and Sammy to join us around four o'clock, if you don't mind?"

Cobwebs still clouded Doug's head.

He fought to rid his mind of them and then focused to concentrate on the phone call. "I'm sorry, but we've already made plans for dinner this evening. Actually it's a special occasion with Jerry and Kely." Doug slid his foot over the edge of the bed for the extra coolness.

"Oh, so that's why they're not available either."

"You've talked to them already this morning?"

"Yes. They offered to come by after nine, but mama can't stay awake that late for two nights in a row."

"Well, that's easy enough to fix. We'll meet for dinner a little earlier and then join you folks by seven. Would that work?" Doug hoped his change of plans would be acceptable with their dinner companions.

"Sure, that would be perfect." Bruno agreed.

"Good. Well, I'd better get moving here before...."

"Excuse me, Doug. There's one last thing. I have an urgent meeting scheduled for eleven o'clock tomorrow morning. Could we hold ours at eight instead of ten?"

Doug strained his memory for possible time conflicts. "I can't think of any problems for the moment. If so, I'll call you after I get into the office tomorrow."

"Great. I'll be seeing you guys tonight, right?"

"Yes, immediately after we've finished with dinner."

Both men said goodbye.

Doug hung up the receiver and closed his eyes.

His mind still struggled with the image of working so

closely with Bruno. It was not that he disliked him or his family. It was just that he had been given no choice about being a part of such a close relationship. Fate had moved his life into places where the choices seemed limited.

He yearned for a brief nap.

Quietly he yawned and remembered what his life had been like last December. He was deeply in love with Catherine, but sadly could not acknowledge it. His occasional weekend trips to Las Vegas were a lot of fun, but they could have been avoided if only he had demonstrated his feelings for her in more loving ways.

That type of commitment was a tough concept for many men to handle although not especially hard to feel or to understand on a superficial level. After all he had been very committed to the marines and to offering unwavering support to all of his jarhead buddies. The strength of that commitment easily led him into life-threatening and quite often extremely deadly situations.

Somehow it seemed like a totally different kind of commitment, but he knew in his gut that it was not. Seeking justification only made it seem that way.

Commitment to a woman, to a potential life-partner seemed to be very different. Actually it was different but in an unusual sort of way. He sought words to explain how it made him feel, but none were available.

Prior to meeting Mr. C, it would have been unthinkable for him to have ever had anything to do with Bruno, let alone work or socialize with him. Memories of that weekend flooded his half-asleep consciousness.

Those events had turned his entire life upside-down.

Doug yawned again and rubbed his drowsy eyes.

A spilled glass of beer, a sick vindictive man with the power of life and death over others made for a terrible combination. It was Mr. C's trying at any cost to get even with him and save face that launched his involvement with the mob. That dangerous man was also one of Bruno's most effective Lieutenants. Doug had cursed that initial encounter with Mr. C a hundred times since then because every one of the encounters that followed became more painful, destructive and deadly.

As he neared sleep, images came quicker.

Doug's eyes moved rapidly.

He remembered the shouting incident in the lobby of *The Golden Phoenix*, the unannounced visit to his room later in the night by Mr. C's goons and the deadly freeway incident. He remembered the first hit attempts in his home, at the Ocean View Motel and then at the hospital, the destruction of his home, the death of innocent people and finally the bloody shoot-out that stole Catherine from him.

Of course he remembered.

It had been burned permanently into his memory more than a hundred times since then. Often tempered with salty tears, but he remembered it all, every ghastly moment. Until finally he had no choice, but to build his courage and take the final battle to Mr. C.

He remembered painfully how he found Mr. C's home, went over the protective wall, dealt with the outside guards, entered the house and eventually confronted Mr. C. He often wondered if he had actually killed Mario and Mr. C at the very moment Catherine had died miles away in the hospital. In a comforting sort of way he wanted it to be true and in his tortured mind it had happened that way.

As regularly happened in his vivid nightmare, Mr. C began firing the TEC-9 at him through the front of the ornate bar. He scrambled the full length behind it to avoid the pounding rain of bullets. Unconsciously his arms and legs relived those frightening few moments.

"Hey, hon. Wake up! It's happening again." Sammy's plea shattered the sleepy morning air. "Come on, Doug. Wake up! You're having that dream again." Trying to avoid his thrashing limbs she struggled to wake him.

"What!" Doug jerked and sprang up in bed.

He knew exactly what had happened and this was not the first time Sammy had experienced the physical side of his terrifying flashbacks that involved his trying to avoid being hit by Mr. C's bullets.

"Are you okay, dear?" Sammy pleaded.

The sound of her voice soothed him. Her unqualified love expressed magic in the ways she spoke, touched and cared for him. She brought far more than natural beauty to their relationship.

"I'm so sorry, sweetheart. Did I hurt you this time?" Doug's hands sought to massage any injuries.

"No, but it still scares the beejebers out of me."

"I know." Doug pulled her naked body closer.

His strong arms enveloped her. Moist lips burrowed into the curve of her neck. He felt her breath softly caress the skin behind his ear. His weight pressed into her softer flesh. She moved ever so slightly to redistribute the pressure resting on her breasts.

Each felt the warmth of the other.

His distress eased. His pounding heart softened. Their legs intermingled gently and neither moved.

Renewed slumber came quickly.

Later Doug awakened feeling he had just experienced a pleasant dream, but his fading memory of it would not return. He looked toward the clock.

It was 8:52 a.m.

Resting on his back, Doug's awareness sought that sliver of time between being awake and being asleep when the mind dwells naturally on the unsettled items in one's past. He knew there were many to be faced. Shortly his growing sense of drowsiness turned to Sammy.

She breathed softly, slowly almost silently. Her head rested on his shoulder. He moved his arm gently until he could easily stroke her waist with two fingers.

The loving movements did not rouse her.

Her breasts pushed playfully into his side. He sensed the warmth. Their erotic touch teased and filled his male ego with a sense of growing passion. One of her legs extended across his. Her arm draped across his chest. Her sculpted goddess-like hand encircled his elbow.

Doug moved to position his lips on her forehead. He paused, planting a silent kiss. She did not stir.

His head rolled back to the pillow and he stared again at the darkened ceiling.

Memories of Sammy were far more pleasant.

He first noticed her three years ago and had recognized her for months at the casino before she ever acknowledged him. He played at her table for a while every day when he visited Las Vegas. Eventually she acknowledged him and they spoke often while he played blackjack.

Samantha Lynn Harper was born in Tucson, Arizona during the early morning of July 30, 1958. Her well-to-do family, innocent beauty and even disposition filled her childhood with wonderful memories. She graduated from the university in 1980 with a degree that over-qualified her to be a housewife and mother, but that, in a secret sort of way, was her only goal in life.

She trusted that life was usually fair and could easily voice an opinion when it was not. Her striking beauty gave her a special strength. She knew as a child that she had power over others, but seldom felt the need to use it.

She married John Wells, a brand-new attorney, the following year and his first job took them to San Francisco. Their son, Samuel, was born the next year and they called him Tadpole. The two of them had answered her dreams for a good life filled with joy.

Once settled John went to work early each morning so that he could be home every evening to spend the extra time with his family. Sammy spent her every waking moment with Tadpole. She nurtured, praised and taught him from the very first day. He toddled easily by week 26, spoke complete baby sentences at the age of seventeen months and read children's books unassisted at the age of three and a half.

Her fairy tale ended the week Tadpole turned five.

John and Tadpole left for the San Francisco Zoo one Saturday morning in June of 1987. Sammy planned to surprise them with a picnic lunch later in the morning, but that police call at 10:46 a.m. tore her life apart.

John and Tadpole had both died in a fiery automobile crash an hour earlier. Sammy's parents and two sisters immediately flew from Arizona to be with her, but none of them could have known that it would not be nearly enough support to ease her mourning.

The funeral was on Tuesday. Her sisters left for home the next day and her parents flew home the following day only after they had extracted a promise from Sammy that she would make an extended trip to visit with them in Tucson the following week.

Sammy drove to the cemetery later that afternoon.

Her tears were heavy and frequent. The anguish was deep and lingered in every part of her body. At the grave she sobbed uncontrollably for hours.

The foggy chill of the evening air went unnoticed. The pain of her immense loss veiled her face that night and stole secretly into her heart.

Around midnight she awoke with her arm still draped over Tadpole's grave. She had fallen asleep astride John's grave. Late night dew had moistened her clothes. She shivered from the cold and also from the realizations that she was now alone. She felt as if her life had ended too.

Graveside soil smudged her face and buried the pain of death deep in her eyes. After a lingering tearful goodbye she climbed into her '86 Dodge station wagon and drove North, not caring where she went.

A week later she stopped in a little town in Oregon and closed her checking account. She took everything in cash. She now had $4,243.09 in her purse.

In January of 1988 Sammy arrived in Las Vegas with only faint memories of the past six months, where she had been and what she had done. She paid a week's rent for a cheap motel, bought a new dress, walked into a casino, applied for a job and was hired on the spot.

After getting her new outfit she was broke, but she

knew she would have a warm bed to sleep in for the next week. For the moment any planning beyond that short period of time was too difficult.

Doug noticed her several weeks later. She had....

Sammy stirred, quickly drawing his attention to her.

The digital clock now indicated the time to be 9:23. She rolled onto her back adjusting the sheet and peeked at him with bright blue eyes.

She slowly yawned, but tried to hide it, then stretched well-rested arms above her head.

He met her big-eyed gaze with a smile.

She returned it.

Doug spoke. "Look at this. You're awake early."

"What do you mean...?"

"It's not lunch time yet, so...."

"Cut it out, Doug. I don't like it when you tease me like this and make fun of how much I like to sleep."

"Well, what would you rather I do?"

"I'll show you."

Sammy pressed a button on the clock radio.

Soft music began playing. With her foot she pushed the sheet to the end of the bed. She reached for the side of Doug's head and pulled him into a warm, moist kiss.

They embraced flesh against flesh.

Doug rolled to his side then rested lightly on Sammy. His foot slid between hers. Her feet moved apart.

Their passion grew to the repetitive sounds common in so many of the '60's love songs.

📖

For most of the night Townsen steamed about the death of Gilberto Leone, but each of Harris' men swore that he was killed in self-defense. Shortly after the coroner's pictures were taken Harris and his men left the scene.

Officer Reynolds provided the only written statement. In disgust Townsen had read the incident report over and over. He read it again.

I was escorting a male suspect for transport to the West LA Station. Suspect walked several steps ahead of me with Detective Harris and Officer Garcia walking ahead of him. As we neared the transport vehicle, the suspect stopped and without warning turned suddenly. Before I could react or even issue a verbal warning the suspect withdrew something from under his jacket. With him facing me, I observed a shinny object in his hand and believed it to be a chrome-plated revolver. Suspect raised and pointed it directly at me. Believing that the suspect was preparing to shoot me, I drew my side arm and fired twice at him. Suspect was pronounced dead at the scene.

Something did not smell right with the statement. He knew it was a lie, but had no way of ever proving it. Feeling his desperation grow, he tossed it on the table.

Earlier he had placed several calls to Harris' office, but had not been able to reach him. He decided that if he continued to get no answer during the next hour in his office he would try calling him at home.

He reached for the phone again and dialed the number.

As the phone rang this time, someone answered it.

"Harris here."

"Harris, what the hell really happened with Leone last night?" Townsen yelled.

"Who is this?" Harris shouted.

"This is Agent Townsen. Just what kind of shit are you trying to pull with this stunt?"

"Get a grip, Townsen."

"Listen, Mister. I don't believe Reynolds' lying statement for one second, so are you going to come clean with me about what really happened there?"

"God-damn it, Townsen, since you weren't even with us just back off."

Again Townsen shouted. "Don't fuck with me, Harris. I know Reynolds shot that man in cold blood. Now are you going to tell me about it or do I have to nail your ass right along with his!"

"Hold on a minute. You don't seem to understand anything about what's happening here, Townsen."

"Well, why don't you just bump me a little further up the learning curve with some friggin' details."

"First off, there's one less scumbag working the streets this morning. That fact alone ought to get Reynolds a fifty thousand-dollar a year raise because he saved taxpayers a couple of million dollars. This guy was...."

"Harris, that's a crock a shit and you know it! Who do you think you're talking to, some rookie?"

"Look. What's the big deal?" Harris ranted.

"For one thing I wanted to nail Bruno Sebastino in the flesh and your juvenile antics have probably screwed that up big time for me."

"Get real, Townsen. If your case against anyone in the mob depended on that small fry, then you don't deserve to ever catch bigger fish."

"Where do you get your dumb-ass information?"

"What do you mean? That guy was a nobody, a flunky, a jerk-off, a…."

"Harris. You're pathetic. For your information Mr. Gilberto Leone was the heir apparent to the LA Mafia Chair. He's been Bruno Sebastino's life-long best friend in the whole damn world, even from childhood!"

"Are you shitting me, Townsen? Where did you come up with that delectable jewel?"

"That's my job! What do you think I use a magic pet rock or something like that?"

"Hey, I'm sorry. I didn't know. None of us knew."

"It looks like your snitch's story about Bruno being at that club was also a big crock."

"Hey, I don't make it up, Mister. I just report it. Better luck next time, if you know what I mean."

Townsen could no longer stomach Harris' arrogant attitude. He wanted to scream at him, but decided it was wise to end the conversation with another warning.

"Harris, keep your boy, Reynolds, in check."

He slammed the phone onto the cradle.

📖

Harris left his office at 11:30 for lunch. Several blocks from the precinct he stopped at a pay phone and dialed his contact inside one of the LA Mafia families.

The man answered. "Yeah."

"Harris here. The first phase is done. You might have seen some of the details on the morning news."

"I saw it. Did you take out Bert as a bonus for me?"

"Certainly. If you're planning to be in a position to move up in the business when this operation is over then my clearing the way for you ought to be worth a little something extra."

"That it is, Jason, that it is."

"I've got one more meeting with Mr. Sebastino scheduled during lunch tomorrow to see if I can get approval for moving our plans off the starting line. If that fails again I'll move onto phase two, so that you'll be in a better position to eventually make those kinds of serious decisions."

"I hope you're right about all of this, Jason. Are you aware that if a single word ever leaks out about our discussions, we're both going to be very dead?"

"You play it straight, Marty. I'll handle all of that."

"You've got it, Jason."

Chapter Four

"Bert and I go back to, well, around 1928 or so." Bruno's voice broke as he recalled those playful times with his dearly departed friend.

Jay nodded as he fought an urge to yawn. "That's considerably longer than most people have been alive." Jay had listened to Bruno's reminiscing for more than an hour now. It was just past noon and it appeared that Bruno would revisit those early years yet again.

Their elegantly prepared lunch was now cold, picked at around the edges and mostly uneaten.

"I know, Jay. I was almost five. It was just a couple of weeks until my next birthday and he was a year or so younger. We spent every day during those silly childhood years together in the alley between our tenements. We played and hid for hours in the sewers, ran up and down the stairs endlessly and climbed on the roofs like they were mountaintops to be explored."

Bruno smiled at the images.

"Those were my carefree days." He added.

"We even had our own telephones made out of a ball of string and some old tin cans strung between the two buildings. I'll bet you didn't ever do anything like that. I remember that we each stole our first kiss from the same neighborhood girl, Anna."

He paused to reflect on that special event.

"You know this is the first time I'm unable to remember her complete name, but Bert and I fought over her for the next twelve years. She became a nurse and went to England in 1939. She died in the Nazi Blitz of London."

Bruno stopped to wipe his nose and eyes.

"This will certainly not be remembered as one of your better days." Jay consoled believing that he should say as little as possible at a time like this.

"That's for sure." He felt the discomfort in Jay's voice then he asked. "Are you trying to cheer me up?"

They just stared at each other.

Finally Bruno smiled.

Jay commented. "Not really, I was just wondering why Bert would ever pull such a dumb stunt as that."

Bruno shook his head. "I don't know, but that certainly doesn't sound very much like him."

"That's pretty much how I'm thinking about it."

"Well, I've been giving it a lot of thought and personally I just can't find a way to believe it. Bert would never have done such a damn foolish thing as pulling a gun on a cop. No way! In fact now that I think about it, Bert didn't usually even carry a gun, much less a chromed one. That's

why he hired a bodyguard. So how th
done any of what Detective Harris accus

Bruno's attitude changed with every n
tered. His anger grew and his temperature
know, Jay. They killed him! There's no doub   at it.
That's what they did. That's exactly what that son-of-a-
bitch Harris did. Those bastards killed Bert."

Jay nodded. "I think you're right. But why?"

"I don't know, but something just didn't sound quite
right last night when Detective Harris gave us the *bad
news*, as he called it."

Bruno picked up a single pitted olive from his lunch
plate and lingered with his thoughts. After popping it into
his mouth he chewed it twice and swallowed it.

"You know, Bruno, that's it. His lack of professional-
ism is what gives him away."

Nodding Bruno spoke. "I agree with that. He commis-
erated with us far too much, didn't he? It was all the FBI's
fault. It was this reason or it was that problem, he said.
Someone else failed to check him properly before taking
him to the station. It was always someone else. There were
just too many unbelievable excuses. Just plain lame is the
best way to describe it, I think"

"That's right. He worked way too hard to persuade us
of the unusual details surrounding Bert's death. I learned
years ago to be suspicious of stories that manage to cover
all the angles. Detective Harris is some character, isn't
he?" Jay added.

"That's for sure. He's been after me to put him back on
the payroll ever since Fred went out of business last winter, but I wouldn't."

"So what's the problem?"

"He's just an *empty suit*. A few months ago he had a plan that would get us involved in *hi-tech piracy*. He made it sound way too easy for the big percentage he wanted for himself. The money was all that seemed to matter to him. The planning was all left to us. He didn't seem to have much of himself invested in the plan. He has no loyalties, not to me, his precinct and not even to his wife. That kind of man gives me poor reasons to trust what he says."

"That would make me suspicious, too."

"Besides that he wasn't reliable with his channeling of useful info. Fred was concerned about him from the get-go. Other informants convinced us that he sanitized much of the info he passed on to us."

"Do you think he's playing both sides of the fence?"

Bruno paused. "Well, not exactly. It seems like he was only working with us for the money he could collect and I want more from those I have to deal with. He only gave us just enough info to get paid and that was it."

"Oh...."

"His lack of loyalties makes for a dangerous man in my book, especially if he gets too much inside info."

"Have you taken any steps to protect yourself?"

"Nothing out of the ordinary. I've simply refused to let him get too involved with anything. He's coming to lunch on Monday and I expect him to be a very good boy. If he doesn't, I'll have two extra guards there to watch us."

"That's smart until you can figure out his agenda."

"Exactly, and that's what has me puzzled, Jay."

"I see what you mean. He wants a job from you and your best friend gets murdered in his presence when you fail to give him one. It looks like there might be a lot more to this situation than first meets the eye."

Bruno leaned forward. "Hmmm, sounds interesting, Jay. Where are you going with this?"

"Well, because of your connections downtown, there is only a limited number of things he can do to get at you legally. So, he goes for something that will, and then he does it, in a very personal way I might add."

Bruno leaned back in his chair. "I see what you mean. It seems clear that he's up to something else. I'll put the word out to keep a watchful eye on him."

Jay nodded. "That would be a smart move."

Bruno picked up the telephone on a nearby table.

📖

Doug jumped in his sleep.

He awoke instantly, but with no memory of his dream. He stared at the ceiling to focus his eyes. He glanced toward Sammy. She rested on her shoulder facing away from him. The sheet was pulled to her neck. Blond hair formed a mound on her pillow.

He moved closer.

She breathed lightly.

Only the briefest of movement occurred in her shoulder. He paused to await another, but none came. He gently slid the sheet to her waist. One of her arms extended over the edge of the bed. The other curled inward until her fingers enclosed a soft, round breast.

At thirty-two her body retained its youth and suppleness. His eyes greatly appreciated the sight of her.

Doug's arm encircled her, coming to rest on her hand. He thought about the pleasures they had shared. He thought about their future together. His lips rested on the upper part of her back. He closed his eyes hoping to savor the warm moment, but as slumber came it did not last.

The sound of rapid gunfire from Mario's Uzi discharged in Doug's mind. He watched as the windshield of Catherine's car exploded from the blast and she fell to the ground mortally wounded.

His heart ached from the memory.

Her warm blood drenched his clothing. Tears rolled off his cheeks as her life and their future flowed along the street and into the gutter. He loved Catherine, but he had hesitated because of his fear of a commitment.

Today he loved Sammy, but now he hesitated because of his reoccurring pain. Several times during the day painful images from the past stole into his mind.

The pleasure and joyful companionship he received from Sammy were insufficient to rid him of the torment he felt, but he hoped they eventually would.

Sammy stirred. Doug's mind returned to the present.

"Hey, Doug. Loosen your grip a bit, you're squeezing me too hard." She complained.

Doug relaxed. "I'm sorry. Are you okay?"

"I'll probably have another bruise, but I'm fine now."

She rolled toward him.

Their lips met in a quick kiss.

Doug moved, allowing her to lie flat on the bed.

She sighed and turned her head toward him. "I suppose I should get some work done on those new drawings. Do you mind if I take a few hours out of our time for that?"

He nodded. "No, not at all. I should be able to find a college game on the tube this afternoon to keep me occupied." He thought of the dynamite evening dress she had worn the night before and how she had labored with the drawings to design it and then with the fabric to tailor it.

"Good. I only need to do a few more sketches for that December show and I'll be done for the day."

She smiled at her thoughts and stared at the ceiling. In the past Doug had seen her in this contemplative mood and he enjoyed seeing her there. She sought these brief forays into the clothing design world and her growing talent was becoming apparent to most who had glimpsed her work.

After a couple of minutes she said. "I'm starved. You ready for some chow, Mr. Carlson?"

"Sure. Are you planning to cook or will this be another champagne brunch at *The Waterfront*?"

Jokingly she responded. "What do you think?"

📖

By 1:30 Bruno had finished his lunch.

Jay had departed earlier in the afternoon to spend some time on the golf course. Left with his thoughts, Bruno continued to recall shared childhood antics with Bert. Occasionally tearful moments arrived. After each one Bruno wiped his eyes, took a sip of spring water with a slice of lemon and moved to the next waiting memory.

Distracted by playful sounds, Bruno rose to find the source of the laughter. Down the hall from his sitting room was one of the children's playrooms.

It sounded like someone had accidentally left the door

ajar. As he approached, the gaiety grew. He entered and saw Emily and Rebecca, his two granddaughters, ages six and nearly four, playing across the room.

"What's this, two beautiful pooh bears?" He asked.

The girls giggled with delight. He approached them and knelt with massive arms outstretched.

They ran into them.

"Papa!" They each exclaimed with glee.

"Are you two busy gathering honey for dinner?"

"Of course not, Papa. We did that earlier today." Emily explained. She often spoke for her younger sister.

"Well, why are you both so excited?"

They giggled again.

Emily sought to control herself and was finally able to speak through her remaining laughter. "I was telling Beck the story of how baby birds learn to fly."

Again they burst into intense laughter. By now they each had an arm around their grandfather's neck.

Bruno joined their laughter without feeling the same level of humor. "Maybe I should hear that sometime."

He hugged and kissed each girl, then stood.

"This has been a nice visit, but I have to get back to my chores. I hope you two have a fun afternoon."

The girls went back to their play.

Bruno closed the door behind him and returned to his easy chair. Now it was quiet. He focused on his dear departed friend again.

His grieving process was taking its intended course.

📖

Kely and Jerry's favorite evening spot was *The Sandalwood Café and Restaurant* at the end of the Santa Monica Pier. They preferred dining on the lower deck if the chill of the ocean breeze allowed it.

So far the afternoon had been made to order for just that. The limo picked them up at 4:15. Twenty minutes later Sammy and Doug were picked up. The leisurely drive across town afforded them time to relax, have a quick refreshment and share the happenings of their day.

Arriving at a restaurant and exiting from a limousine usually draws the attention of onlookers. Jerry and Kely were unfazed by it. Sammy was becoming accustomed to it, but Doug was too easily embarrassed and he was certain that everyone knew it was Bruno's limousine.

Once seated at their table Doug spoke to Jerry. "What kind of brew would you like this evening, bro?"

"If it's ice-cold, I don't really care. Tonight I've got bigger things on my mind." Jerry teased.

Everyone's eyes turned to him in anticipation.

Picking up his menu he ignored them through a sly lingering smile. Sammy and Kely exchanged looks of pleasant confusion. Doug ordered drinks around the table before the hostess left them.

Doug sat across the table from Kely. Their eyes flirted briefly. She held a very special place in his heart.

If she had not been Catherine's younger sister and so many other things had not happened, he might have fallen in love with her years before she ever met Jerry.

Sadly, she was there when Catherine had died.

Those were painful days for each of them, but they held onto each other as brother and sister and shared the grieving of their mutual loss.

They also shared an ocean cruise to celebrate Catherine's love of life and discovered that while their love for one another was indeed strong, it could never grow into a satisfying romantic one.

Doug sipped his beer and recalled that afternoon on the third day of the cruise. He and Kely had gone ashore and rented a *mini-moke* on the island of Barbados.

The dune buggy shaped third-world vehicle took them entirely around the island in only a few hours. Late in the morning they stopped at a tattered grocery store to buy hard rolls, soft cheese and cold drinks.

A few miles later they pulled off of the main road and onto the beach where they parked. Doug opened the drinks and Kely sliced their lunch.

Her bikini and modest cover caught his eye.

Soon seductive images of Catherine mixed closely with those of Kely kneeling before him.

His heart ached painfully for his lost love. He stared longingly at her as his emotions grew into passion.

When she finished, she set a plate between them. Their eyes met briefly and became fixed on each other.

The mid-day sun was hot.

Their hands met almost as if by chance on the sandy towel. The sound of tropical birds playing in the distance mixed with the roar of ocean waves on the baking sand. Through mutual stares her other hand found and lightly caressed his forearm.

With locked searching eyes they leaned back on the beach towel. Doug's hand touched the radiant heat of her slender side. The magic of his passion was transferred to her. She rolled to her back.

His hand caressed her stomach.

She closed her eyes to savor the sensation.

Doug laid his head gently on her chest.

Hot smooth hands and arms lightly encircled him. His arm slid under her neck. His head moved slowly upward, past her neck and chin.

Her lips instinctively tendered two moist kisses.

Again peering deep into their passionate eyes both of their shattered hearts melted. A brief moment of tenderness surrounded them. Their shared pain was lifted.

Lonely lips were quenched.

Loving caresses were exchanged.

Within seconds the sound of a nearby seagull brought it to an end. Doug raised his head and whispered. "I love you, but we need to speak of this before we can move on."

She placed her head next to his and asked. "Just let me hold you for a moment."

She pulled him close.

He complied.

Each felt the heat offered by the other's embrace. Their body sweat mixed and dripped to the towel. Their healing had finally begun. Each felt it happening. The non-sexual joy of the moment filled them.

After hundreds of shared heartbeats they relaxed.

Now lying on the towel they looked to the sky. Blue and white tones mixed randomly to allow most of the sun to shine through a haze.

Kely remembered Doug's earlier comment and said. "I love you too, but this day is for *Katy*."

After a long pause Doug whispered. "I know. I haven't

heard you use that nickname for her all week."

She began to sob. "I couldn't. Just knowing that she's gone hurts too much. I wanted to be here like this for just a moment for her, for you and for me."

"I'm glad." His hand sought hers and squeezed.

"Doug, tell me how much you loved Katy."

"More than anything." Doug felt a tear flow.

"I'm glad she found love with you before she died."

Unable to speak for a moment, he just nodded.

Sensing that Doug was lost in thought, Sammy moved her chair closer to him and smiled.

He hurried to finish his recollections.

Today the touch of Kely's smile reminded him that he remained a cherished part of her deepest thoughts. As she smiled and spoke to Jerry, Doug released his memories of that day on the beach.

"Okay, honey. What do you have planned for us this evening?" Kely's hand reached for Jerry.

"Yeah, Mr. Sebastino. We'll have no secrets at this table." Sammy added mockingly through a wide smile.

Jerry ignored them as he peered into the open menu he held. Doug jumped into the banter to assist him.

"Okay, Ladies, give the man a break! Let's get some alcohol into him first. I'm sure that'll loosen his tongue and then you can have your way with him."

Jerry failed to maintain his stoic demeanor and grinned at them across the table. "The three of you make it very hard for a man to keep an important surprise."

Kely seemed to anticipate what might be occurring.

Sammy's hand jumped to cover her mouth.

Doug smiled in silence since he already knew what

Jerry had planned to do that evening.

Without waiting any longer, Jerry pushed his chair aside to kneel before Kely.

Her eyes grew large. Sammy squealed in delight.

Doug's hand reached for Sammy.

Jerry took both of Kely's hands into his. Her smile faded ever so slightly as she awaited the big moment.

"Kely, my dear, you are the warmth in my every sunrise. You are the reason I live and breathe each day. You are the joy of my nights. You are the woman I choose to love for the rest of my life and to raise my family. I love you very much."

Kely was frozen in the moment.

Sammy smiled broadly through growing anticipation. Several adjacent diners stopped to watch and to enjoy the proposal. Jerry's hand slipped into his coat pocket to retrieve a small white ring case.

He opened it, smiling as he presented it to Kely.

Her face glowed.

"My darling, I would like you to accept this ring as a symbol of my deep love and as a daily reminder of my life long commitment to you." He paused.

"Kely Elizabeth Walker, will you marry me?"

Chapter Five

"How long can you sustain this spectacular level of revenue, Doug?" In business meetings Bruno's voice usually rang loud, full of unending comments and often quite authoritarian. This particular one had been filled with more than enough extremes.

"Well, in theory I believe there is an absolute limit, but I don't think we'll bump into it for sometime yet, maybe a year, maybe a little less. Then we'll settle for maintaining revenue at that particular point, whatever it is. This controlling assumption is based on the market continuing to grow in step with our current level of trading."

Every weekday morning Doug arrived in his office at 5:00. He liked those early hours because they were so productive and private.

The digital desk clock told him it was now 8:06.

"Okay, if you can add thirty new trading stations without breaking the bank then I authorize you to do it." Bruno gathered the reports that Doug had prepared earlier and scanned them again. He could not believe his eyes.

Doug's infant operation had netted more revenue in two months than all the rest of Bruno's LA operations had netted for him during all of last year. At first Bruno was skeptical, but the regular bank deposits that were being made for him quickly changed his mind.

Doug grinned.

"Good. There's a four-week training period for the new staff, but I'll pay for that. By Halloween, you should be seeing as much as double your normal weekly revenue. Maybe as much as two hundred and fifty million dollars a week if the projections are accurate."

"I don't know how you do it, Doug, but I like it. I like it a lot!" Bruno reached to pat him on the shoulder.

"Well, thank you, Bruno."

"Are you still on the books for only one percent?" Bruno shook his head, feeling that Doug had always accepted far too little for his contribution in the stock investment company.

"Yes, sir."

Doug's thoughts jumped immediately to those early negotiations with Bruno.

Being skeptical about even working for him at first, Doug finally drew the line at working with any of the mob's illegal or dirty money. If there was no clean money to be invested, then he was out of the picture completely.

That was his final negotiating position. Bruno lingered for a long time then smiled broadly as he quickly extended his hand, saying. "Doug, you've got yourself a deal."

Eventually a computer center was established to manage only the funds Doug could verify as being clean. A handful of experienced accountants were transferred to work with him and the growing cash accounts.

Hundreds of thousands of dollars were invested, but the fabulous returns did not justify the outrageous salary Bruno paid him. Shortly afterwards, a day trading department was established and he was pleased to finally earn a percentage of the weekly returns.

"And if you don't mind me asking, Doug, just what does that work out to be for you?"

Leaning back in his chair Doug thought.

"Well, let's see. If we hit the projected two-hundred-and-fifty it will be around three million a week for me."

"Doug, if I could have made this kind of money when I was a young man, I wouldn't have busted so many heads over the years. I would have become a much different man today. How did you ever work all of this stuff out?"

"It was strictly observation, sir. I simply paid close attention to how the financial markets really worked, then stopped listening to the BS from so-called experts about how one should invest to make money in the market. With enough cash focused into certain areas, highly profitable results can be had on a regular and consistent basis."

"Well, Doug. I'm pleased with the returns from your new company. It's hard to believe that I'm becoming so dependent on a legal business that has magically earned almost a billion dollars in only a few short months."

With a smile Doug added. "In a year you won't have to rely on any of your current businesses because of this staggering level of revenue."

"And you'd like me to divest some or all of them?"

"Well, that is an idea worth some of your concentrated thought. Retirement might be a nice thing for you to consider at this particular point in your life. Who knows, an easier life might make for a longer one."

Bruno laughed.

"You and Jerry are certainly a lot alike. He says some of the very same things. Are the two of you working on a plan to make me go totally legit?"

"It's only logical when you stop to think about it. Why should you dodge the law and take risks when they aren't necessary for you to have a very nice lifestyle? Already you are a very rich man and with my help getting much richer every day."

"That's exactly what Kely said. Are all of you guys in a conspiracy against me?"

Imitating a Jimmy Cagney character from a classical movie, Doug responded. "You don't think I'm going to rat on them, do you?"

Both men laughed.

The meeting was over so their conversation turned to other more personal matters.

Bruno asked. "Did Sammy catch the company jet to Las Vegas this morning?"

"Yes, she called me just before it took off." Doug looked at his watch. "It should have landed by now."

Doug's mind wandered to pleasant thoughts of Sammy and to the unusual problem they faced in the early days of their courtship.

Sammy was always well informed about who owned *The Golden Phoenix Hotel and Casino*. She knew that she worked for the mob. That was okay, but she refused to be a part of their other less legal activities.

She declined to be one of their party girls although the money and perks were fabulous. Instead she did her regular shift, earned her money honestly and then went home each evening to build her new life.

Sometimes she cried about her losses in the past. At other times it was a growing uncertainty about the future that brought tears. After a while, the painful emotion behind her tears was finally gone.

Shortly after the incident with Mr. C was concluded, Doug and Jerry became close friends. Soon they partied together in the Las Vegas casino every other weekend.

Initially Sammy refused to associate with Doug away from her table, but as the facts about his nonmember status in the mob accumulated, she relaxed trusting that he was not engaged in any of their illegal or distasteful activities.

Their romance, once started, was out of control and grew like a raging forest fire.

Bruno's next comment brought Doug back from his daydreaming. "That's good. You've got yourself a damn fine woman there, son."

"I know. She's so good at simply reaching out to softly touch and influence others. I…."

The authoritarian side of Bruno interrupted him. "So, when are you going to make her stop working those long hours at the casino?"

Doug shook his head and chuckled. "Like I could really do that. If she's not willing to stop on her own then she won't leave, no matter what I say or do."

"I don't understand how you young men of today can

live with these headstrong women. In my day they would have never attempted such things."

"Well, Bruno, this is a new day. Lots of things are much different than you would remember."

"I suppose." Bruno looked at his watch, as he nodded. "Well, for now I've got to get downtown for a meeting and then back home for a luncheon date."

Excitement grew in Doug's face as he prepared to ask. "There's one last thing I wanted to mention before you go. I just read about an obscure group of computer professionals around the world putting together a network of computers. They're expanding an older system to include business and government computers linked to those already installed at a number of universities around the world."

Bruno leaned forward as if intrigued by the concept. "And the overall plan of this group is to do what?"

"Well, with so many computer projects like this there's usually a lot more promised than can actually be delivered. However, the ultimate goal seems to be for extending these electronic links into homes and then disbursing information twenty-four hours a day to anyone who might want it during those odd hours."

"This sounds intriguing, but I can't see any useful way for me to use it, can you?" Bruno started to stand.

"Well, assuming that the growth trends of the past ten years continue for another five, there will be enough home based computers around the world to make it finally practical. When a vast number of computers are connected by telephone links like this, the way many companies do their business will probably be changed overnight. I think we can count on something like this happening by the middle of the decade, if not sooner."

"Interesting, but I've got to run. Will you keep me posted on this? What did you say this group was called?"

Not having an answer Doug rubbed the back of his neck as he thought about it. "I don't actually know. It's just an *inter*connected *net*work for now." He shook his head. "I don't think there's a name for it yet."

"I'm beginning to see how the power and the special capabilities of these computers make the unheard of technologies grow. With any expanded involvement by business and government it's clear to me that anyone who messes around with the delicate balance these computers require is asking for trouble everywhere they turn."

Bruno stood, they shook hands and walked to a security door. After saying goodbye Doug headed back to his desk. One of his employees approached.

"Excuse me, Mr. Carlson."

Doug halted and turned to face one of his senior office staff. "Yes, Peter?" He asked.

"I have the latest status report, sir. At 38% of the trading day we've made 47% of our expected revenue."

"Excellent, Peter. Is Barry still sick?" Peter nodded and Doug responded. "That's pretty good for only having twenty-nine traders."

"Well, sir. There are actually only twenty-seven. Two of the others were arrested Saturday night at *The Neon Phoenix* and they're still being held in jail."

Nodding, Doug said. "That's better for the revenue, but what's the hold-up on getting them released?"

"I'm not sure exactly. Something about them having unresolved traffic citations and their becoming arrest warrants from the DMV."

"See what you can do to help get them released."

Doug's telephone rang in the distance.

He sprinted to answer it. "Hello. This is Doug."

"Good morning, Mr. Carlson. This is Otis Townsen, FBI Special Operations Division."

Through his surprise, Doug responded. "Well, you're about the last person I'd ever expect to call. What's on your mind this morning, Mr. Townsen?"

"It's been a while since we talked. I thought…."

"Hold on. We were never much for socializing or developing small talk, so get to the point, will you?"

"Are you still sore about that mob deal last year?"

"Look, I'm not sore. Can we get on with this call?"

"Mr. Carlson, my men saved your butt more than once so I expect a little more out of you now, okay?"

"Hey, I'm still on the phone, but you're not talking."

"I want to meet with you in person later this afternoon. Where can we meet?" Townsen's voice demanded.

"What's the topic of our discussion?"

"Your boss and your unusual job."

"And just what does that mean?"

"It's nothing really, just some procedural things. I have a few simple questions about the kind of work you do, who you work for and the very large amounts of money you're putting into your bank account each week. Now that's not too hard for you to handle, is it?"

"No, but why is there a sudden interest in my bank account?" Doug asked.

"I've already told you. It's just some routine matters I want to clear up, starting with you."

"Okay. Be at my office at 5:30 this afternoon."

"What about your staff, will they still be there?"

"No. They're usually out of here by three o'clock."

"That's one of my first questions. What's with the odd working hours you have?"

"Well, Agent Townsen, you'll find that out this evening. Do you know how to get here?"

"Yes."

"Good. Be here at 5:30. Come alone."

📖

Detective Jason Harris drove his late-model brown police-issue vehicle through the arched, landscaped entrance of Bruno's estate. For the last nine months he had tried to setup this meeting.

Since the death of Mr. C, he was officially off of the mob's payroll. Losing those extra twenty-five hundred dollars a month was a loss he had missed and hoped to replace several times before.

He moved along the finely manicured grounds toward the fork in the driveway where he turned to the right. The majestic lines of the home peered through the fall-clad greenery. Earthen colors draped across the stately structure and accented its lines.

The overall size of the house came into view.

Harris gasped.

His vehicle stopped under the covered entrance near the front door. He looked around, scoping out nearby windows, but no one was there.

Harris opened the car door and stood beside it.

He felt the uneven surface of the driveway, scanned the exotic surroundings and wondered if Bruno really appreciated all of this luxury. He adjusted his tie and walked to the door. He spit his chewing gum into an expensive ceramic pot holding an unusual imported plant.

He rang the doorbell.

Carlos admitted Harris and immediately escorted him to the downstairs meeting room where he would have lunch with Bruno.

There was silence as they walked.

Harris followed while noticing at least a half a dozen pieces of expensive art.

Stopping just inside of the door Carlos spoke. "Sir, Mr. Sebastino had been temporarily detained. He should arrive shortly. May I prepare a drink for you?"

He motioned for him to enter and then sit anywhere in the spacious room.

Harris noticed that the room had its own bar. "No thank you. I'll just help myself if you don't mind."

"Very well, sir. Please make yourself comfortable."

Carlos bowed and exited.

The windows on one wall offered a westerly exposure. A covered walkway along the back of the estate shielded it from the heat of the midday sun. The other walls presented a collection of family photos spanning the past thirty years.

A table elegantly set for two, waited adjacent to a window. Several leather chairs, tables and reading lamps were positioned around the fireplace with a fluffy brown bearskin rug in the middle. A desk accompanied by several decorative chairs filled the next corner.

A fully stocked bar beckoned him from the remaining

corner. Harris moved toward it and surveyed its expensive inventory. He settled on whisky straight up, broke the seal on a new bottle and poured himself a half-inch of liquid into a Manhattan glass.

He gulped it and poured another.

Grabbing the glass and bottle, he moved to an over-stuffed chair in front of the fireplace. He leaned back and closed his eyes. Images of living his life in such luxurious surroundings flooded his thoughts.

He smiled, felt his body sink into the soft chair and took a long deep breath. Finally he could relax.

If his meeting went well, it would continue.

He sighed.

Harris' mind wandered to that vacation cabin near Lake Arrowhead he had hoped to buy, that new car for Pam and a fishing boat like the one Sam had recently bought. There were many more things he wanted, but he simply could not afford to get them unless Bruno would accept and pay him for his access to information.

Losing track of time Harris poured and consumed several more drinks. He was nearly asleep when a servant roused him by wheeling a serving cart into the room.

Out of her sight, Harris looked toward the young woman and shouted. "Hey, is Mr. Sebastino here yet?"

Startled, she turned to face him. "Yes, sir. He just arrived and will be here to lunch with you momentarily."

He thanked her and returned his empty glass to the bar. He leaned clumsily on a barstool as Bruno walked quickly into the room followed by two of his bodyguards and several more servants.

"Forgive me, Detective Harris. I apologize for being so

late. I trust that you've been comfortable?"

He offered an open hand. Harris responded likewise.

"Yes, everything's been just fine. I've been enjoying the beauty and comfort of your fireplace."

"Good. Shall we take our seats?" Bruno motioned toward the waiting table.

"Certainly." Harris felt his actions were awkward.

Each man moved to take his seat.

A servant assisted Harris. The guards stood several feet away on opposite sides of the table, watching the diners but not staring directly at them.

The chef filled each plate with manly portions from the serving cart. Harris surveyed the steamy food while Bruno briefly observed something in the back yard.

They began eating. Neither man spoke except to compliment the taste of the food and praise the chef's remarkable culinary talent.

Midway through his entrée Bruno spoke in a firm voice. "Well, Detective Harris, are there any more details about the circumstances of Bert's death?"

"No, I'm afraid not. According to the records I've seen, it's classified as a clear-cut case of self-defense. I don't think I'll be able to alter any of those facts without getting a lot of static from the brass."

"So, there will be no inquiry as to why he still had a gun on him after he had been taken into custody?"

Harris shook his head. "I don't think so since the investigation is being handled by the feds and they are not being very cooperative with it."

"I see. What do you think happened, Mr. Harris?"

"Well, I think someone got sloppy and their lack of attention to their job caused your friend to pay a huge price with his life."

"What about the officer who shot him?"

For a moment Harris was startled that Bruno continued this line of questions. "Officer Reynolds? He's a good man and a damn fine officer. He's a rookie, young and quite an impressive go-getter. I know he was pretty shook up afterwards. I hear he was ordered to take the next few days off just to recover."

Bruno nodded. "So is he feeling better today?"

A servant took Bruno's empty plate.

"I don't really know. I can't recall that I saw him in the precinct this morning, so I think he's still off."

A young servant stood near Harris waiting for his nearly empty plate. After one final bite he allowed her to take it. When that was done, another servant placed peach tarts in front of each man.

"Mr. Harris, if in the course of your duties you were to discover that someone actually dropped that gun on Bert, would you give that person to me?"

Bruno watched Harris' eyes closely.

"Yes sir, in a New York minute."

Bruno knew that Harris had lied, so he feigned a smile of approval. "I'm pleased to hear that, Detective. Maybe you can answer something else for me as well?"

"Sure, if I can." Harris shifted uncomfortably in his chair and hastily took a sip of water.

"What's with the sudden interest of Law Enforcement in the operations of one of my clubs?"

"You know, I don't have any idea. I didn't get to see many of the details about the raid until the final briefing by the feds. They're playing this one close to the vest, if you know what I mean."

"So, you don't know if anything else like this is being planned, do you?" Bruno queried.

"I haven't heard any scuttlebutt like that, but I'll certainly pass it along, if I do."

"That would be appreciated."

Again Bruno nodded and offered a half-smile. He was getting tired of Harris' lies and double-talk. "Well, I think you've answered all of my questions. Can I be of any help to you today, Detective?"

Harris hesitated. "Well, Mr. Sebastino, I don't know if you remember me, but I once worked for Mr. de Casale before he died last year."

Bruno nodded and leaned back into his chair before he spoke. "Also, I seem to remember that you were the person behind all of those plans to move our business into *hi-tech piracy* a few months ago. Isn't that a bit of a risk for a person in your position?"

Harris nodded and was ready to offer his response when Bruno continued. "Do you understand why I could not allow that type of business to get established as a regular part of our operations?"

Harris nodded before speaking. "Oh, that's not an issue for me anymore. I've given up those ideas. My retirement is getting close and I don't want to jeopardize it with anything that big."

Bruno nodded. "Interesting."

"So, if you could use somebody in my unique position in a way that would not draw a lot of attention to me, I could certainly use the extra cash."

Bruno pondered the request before he spoke. "Let me check with some of my associates downtown. I'll give it some thought and get back with you in a couple of days. Will two-hundred be enough for today's information?"

Harris flashed a big smile. "Yes sir, it will."

Bruno stood and motioned for one of the guards to give him the money. "Good, Mr. Romero will show you to your car, Detective Harris."

Bruno walked rapidly out of the room.

After getting two crisp one hundred-dollar bills Harris stood and followed his escort back to his waiting car.

Chapter Six

Townsen arrived at the computer center in West LA ten minutes early. His driver and Agent Wilson accompanied him to the front door.

Doug met them in the lobby.

"Have you ever been late for any appointment, Agent Townsen?" Doug quipped.

He recognized the agent as one of the men who aided him in the gun battle with Mr. C's goons at Westside Hospital last year and the one who actually saved his life. The man offered no sign of recognition.

"Not since anyone's been keeping track." Townsen joked. He smiled, but his men did not.

"What kind of tour are you looking for, *a quick once over* or the *move in and have your meals delivered*?"

"Why don't you start things rolling and I'll let you know when I've had my fill of the gory details."

"Fair enough."

Doug unlocked a security door by pressing a numeric code and sliding a plastic card key through a slot.

He paused and turned to face Townsen. "I'm sorry, but this tour is for only one, Mr. Special Agent Man."

Townsen looked surprised but turned to speak to his men. "Okay, gentlemen. I'll call when I'm ready to leave."

The men exited to their vehicle and Doug locked the exterior door behind them. He and Townsen went through the security door and it automatically locked behind them.

"Agent Townsen, Let me start by saying that this operation is one-hundred percent legal from the accounting records we keep to the copies of computer software that have been installed on each of our machines. So if you are looking for trash on Mr. Sebastino or the mob you won't find anything like that here."

"If you don't mind, Mr. Carlson, I'll decide that for myself based on what I see."

Townsen looked around the main office.

The larger open room was fifty feet wide and at least a hundred feet long. It was filled with colorful chest-high partitions to enclose fifty workspace cubicles.

The perimeter of the wall was lined with computer monitors, mounted on shelves near the ceiling. The monitors were grouped into sets of four about every ten feet. Each of the groups displayed the same computerized stock market data. They were positioned around the room so that they could easily be seen from any location in the room.

Townsen asked. "By the way have you heard anything about the death of Mr. Gilberto Leone?"

Without thinking about it Doug responded. "Only what

I've read in the newspapers. Why do you ask?"

"No reason, I was just wondering. So where exactly does this tour of yours start?"

"Come to my office. I can explain all of the center's technical operation from there much easier."

"Okay, lead the way."

Townsen scanned the cubicles as they walked.

Their occupants had customized each one to their own personal taste. Pictures of girlfriends, wives and children were prominent. Comic clippings and cartoon characters filled the remaining wall space. The expensive executive chair at every desk accentuated the relaxed and comfortable environment.

As Doug approached his office, his mind raced to determine where he would begin his tutorial. The computer monitors in his office mirrored the exact configuration and layout of the data that was displayed in the prior room.

Doug sat in his chair and spoke. "Pull up that chair behind me. Slide it close, so that you can see everything."

Townsen complied, then responded through a growing puzzlement. "What exactly am I suppose to be seeing?"

Doug paused to take a deep breath before he started. "I operate this center exclusively for Bruno Sebastino with only capital from his legal enterprises. It's a private investment service operating solely for his benefit. My goal is to make him more money legally, than he can make busting heads or conducting business in the usual ways."

Townsen's mouth flew open. "Don't tell me you're actually working this close to that scumbag!"

"And what's the problem with that if the activities are legal and all transactions are completely above board?"

"It's just the idea of working for the mob. It makes my skin crawl. How can you do it? You're smarter than that so why are you doing something as degrading as this?"

"It's the most exciting job I've ever had. Mr. Sebastino makes a lot of money with this company and so do I. Tell me, Agent Townsen, do you have a problem with legally making very large amounts of money?"

"Of course not, but don't you have the slightest reservations about this questionable situation?"

"Sure I do and I'm very diligent about every financial interaction that crosses my desk from Bruno. I certainly don't approve of his other business activities, but that was never the point for me. They're disgraceful, so I refuse to participate in any of them. I even refuse to listen to the gossip they offer about them."

"So now you're on a first name basis with him."

Looking disgusted Doug replied. "Do you want me to continue with this or not?"

"Sure." Townsen shook his head. "But I just don't understand it. How can you say that you only handle clean money? Do you actually have someone who checks all the sources of the cash deposits you receive?"

"Of course, that's how we do it. I have several experienced accountants who do nothing but verify the source of all the incoming funds that we plan to invest."

"Okay, do you mind if I see some of those records?"

"I certainly do. Bruno would have a fit if he knew you were even in here looking at the hardware and he would probably kill anybody involved in opening the books to you or anyone else for that matter.

"If they're legit, what's the problem?"

"For Bruno, I suppose the old ways will suffer for a long time and die a prolonged death."

"Are you worried about allowing me to see the inner workings of his private money machine?"

"A bit. I know you're a determined man, but also a reasonable one. Once you see what's happening here, I hope you'll back-off of your inquiries a little and focus your probing efforts elsewhere."

Townsen laughed. "Carlson, you're impossible! You destroyed a big chunk of his crime organization last year and now he trusts you well enough to handle his personal bank account. I just don't get it! Now you think you'll ply your charm to make me pack it up and leave him alone."

"Not exactly, but once you see the bigger picture, maybe you'll realize that he's not the enemy you once thought him to be. That's not too much to ask is it? Just reconsider things based on any new info I can offer."

"Yes, it is and I doubt very seriously if anything like that would ever happen, but you can proceed a little further with your *dog and pony show*."

Doug shook his head.

"Okay, financial markets are much like a two-edged sword. There's a ton of money to either be made or lost in them. Every day tens of thousands of traders are after that potential profit, but only the smarter and luckier ones are rewarded with big chunks of it. Here in the computer center we gather enough of the right pieces of information to keep us thinking smarter and quicker about the ever-changing direction of the market."

"Last year I remember getting a call from a retirement investment manager who presented me with much the same story."

Excitement began to show on Doug's face. "That was small potatoes compared to what I'll show you here. In all circumstances the stock market has only three things it can do—go up, go down or go sideways. Movements of less than twenty points in either direction don't make money for anybody, but on variations greater than that they do."

"So, you're playing the stock market for the mob?"

"Yes, but much more than that. We don't usually trade individual stocks, but instead focus all our attention on the market averages. Savvy traders locate and monitor specific financial variables and instruments that track the movement of the market very closely, so that the bigger plus or minus movements in price of the averages can be translated into short-term profits.

"Among other stock indices we track, the symbol OEX does that for us very well."

"Does what?"

"Oh, I didn't mean to go so fast. Where did I get ahead of you?" Doug apologized.

"All this talk of instruments, indices and plus or minus moves is way over my head. I don't need to know the how, just the what and why."

Doug's mind raced again for the corrective words.

"Let's see. In a nutshell most people think they can only make money when the market goes up, but that's only half of the story. Seasoned Wall Street investors know that they can usually make money no matter which direction the market moves, as long as it's a good sized move of at least thirty or more points."

"Don't toy with me, Carlson! I know that when you

buy a stock and the price goes down the toilet you lose money unless there's something about stocks I don't really understand? Are you sure this is legal?"

Townsen shook his head, mostly at not understanding what was being said.

"Of course, and that's exactly right, if buying or selling stocks are your only choices for investing, but *trading options* on those same stocks allow you to be both a player in the up side and the down side of the market."

Townsen looked confused. "How's that possible?"

"Options come in two flavors, puts and calls. When the market goes up, *calls increase in value*. When it goes down, *puts increase in value*. Pretty simple, huh?"

"I don't know about that. How come no one has ever talked about this kind of investment stuff before? I've had a number of stock for years and my broker's never mentioned a word about any of this kind of tracking."

"Most average investors don't have the time nor inclination to deal with the risk associated with this type of investment. If you don't do it full-time, you can lose your shirt overnight and that's too much of a risk for most individuals like you."

"And you do all of this full-time for the mob?" He asked as he shook his head.

"No, I do all of this full-time for Mr. Sebastino, that is, myself and eighty-three others do it for him."

Townsen's eyes widened. "You have that many people working for you here?"

"Yes, and I'm planning to double the operation during the next few months."

"I'm impressed, Carlson, but what quantities of cash

are you handling for him?"

Doug halted.

His mind sought words to evaluate Townsen's question. He thought about what Bruno would say or do if he learned that such info had been released. Under the circumstances he decided to provide an answer.

"Bruno seeded the whole operation with twenty-five-million dollars. Sixteen trading days later we made that much money in a single day. Afterwards that amount became our daily target."

"You're shit'n me, Carlson, right?"

Doug shook his head. "I'm afraid not and usually we make much more. Occasionally we don't hit the target, but we always come pretty damn close. Our average profit for the last sixty-seven days of stock trading has been thirty-one point four million dollars per day."

Townsen stood and paced between his chair and the door. "Wow! No wonder he keeps you around."

Doug smiled.

Townsen continued, "So what's your share in this stock market gold mine?"

"I take expenses to run the operation directly off the top, then divide ten percent between myself and the staff. I get one percent and they split the rest depending on their position and job performance levels."

"I'll bet that's a nice pile of change."

"It is."

Doug paused.

"That's it! We're done and you're not going to give me any of the real numbers?"

"You're pushing it, Townsen. Besides they won't do

you any good. I've declared every dime of it on my income taxes and I'm sure Bruno has done the same."

"I know, but you've built this up so much. I'm just curious that's all." Townsen exclaimed.

"Okay, but these pieces of info can never be repeated to any other living soul outside of this office. I've banked almost fourteen million dollars, myself. Bruno's received well over a billion dollars to date."

"God-damn, Carlson, that's just unbelievable."

Doug asked. "Now, let's discuss the issue of you, your people and the bureau backing-off of him a bit."

"Why should I? Bruno Sebastino is still a gangster."

"Townsen, you know better than that. LA has never been anything like the crime-ridden cities of the East Coast where the mob has controlled everything in sight. You know that Bruno and his father were never like that."

"And just what do you know about it, Mister!"

"I know plenty." Doug asserted.

"Yeah, just what your sugar daddy tells you."

Chapter Seven

Dusk painted breathtaking colors across the warm September sky. After dark offshore breezes usually forced temperatures to the low 70's.

That made the fall nights bearable.

Jerry reclined in the soft leather of the limo's rear seat. He had just finished a bottle of beer during the ten-minute drive. He would wait for Doug to open the next one.

As the limousine turned onto Doug's street in West Los Angeles, he ended his mushy conversation with Kely on the car phone.

"Gotta run, honey, but I'll be home by 11:00."

"Okay. I think I'll catch that new Bette Midler flick at the Westlake Theater."

"That sounds like a nice girlfriend movie. Why don't you wait until Saturday and watch it with Sammy?"

"I suggested doing that with her on the phone earlier,

but she expects to be working on some of her drawings that evening." Kely sighed.

"That woman is so talented and dedicated. How did she ever find the time to get started with artsy stuff like that?" Jerry inquired.

"I think she studied it in college and only now has decided to put it to good use. I don't think she plans on being a dealer in the casino for much longer." Kely answered.

"Oh." That was news to Jerry.

"Well, anyway, I should be back home from the flick about twenty minutes before you are."

"Great. Have a good time, puddin' face."

Kely giggled upon hearing his new pet name for her. "Okay, I'll see you then, sweetie."

Jerry hung up the phone as the limo pulled smoothly into the driveway. The porch light near the front door went on. The lights inside the house went off.

Jerry shifted across the seat, making room for Doug.

Shortly, the chauffeur opened and held the door.

Doug slid into the car and smiled. "Hey, pal. How you been?" The chauffeur closed the door and returned silently to his driving duties.

"Not too bad. Did you have a good day?"

"Yeah, it was pretty good. I had a visitor this afternoon at the center, Otis Townsen, that federal agent."

Jerry looked puzzled. "What was on his mind?"

"Who knows? I think he was on a fishing expedition for more trash on your dad."

"Did you tell him anything?" Jerry reached into the mini-fridge for a cold beer. He offered one to Doug. They each opened their bottle and took a long sip.

Doug settled into the plush padded seat. "What's there to tell? I just showed him around the center and discussed what we did with the daily trading."

"Did papa approve the tour?"

"No, but there was nothing for Townsen to see."

"Well, I'd be concerned if I were in your shoes. You know how protective papa can be of his privacy. Do you intend to tell him?"

"Sure. I'll do that when we get to the warehouse."

The conversation continued on several topics that these close friends shared—local sports team gossip, the pending wedding, a new restaurant Jerry had recently discovered near the beach, a weekend trip they planned for next month. After ten minutes both men sat in silence, occasionally sipping their beer.

The Coleman Street warehouse was still another fifteen minutes away. Doug's thoughts turned to Sammy and recollections surrounding their first real date.

It was mid-February before Doug felt like returning to Las Vegas for the weekend. By then his friendship with Jerry had flourished. Jerry's romance with Kely sprouted easily the month before and Doug began to feel like the third wheel during dinner, movies and the other outings the three of them attended together.

During their visits to *The Golden Phoenix*, Doug and Jerry usually traveled without dates, expecting to do a bit of serious womanizing for the three-day weekend. Doug did not expect what happened when he and Sammy next came face to face.

Her current shift began at 11:00 p.m.

Doug and Jerry played roulette at a nearby table until

time for her break. As a replacement dealer took her table, they approached. She spotted them and walked in the other direction. They followed her toward the employee lounge.

Once they were off the main floor, Doug spoke to her from a distance. "Hey, Sammy. How you been?"

She paused, looked toward him and continued walking.

Doug spoke again. "What's the matter? Don't you remember me from last year?"

Stopping in her tracks, she turned and waited for the two men. When they stopped in front of her, she spoke directly to them. "Of course, I remember you, Mr. Carlson, and you too, Mr. Sebastino."

With raised eyebrows Doug glanced at Jerry then back into the chill of Sammy's eyes. Looking confused, Jerry shrugged at the strange happenings, turned away and took several steps before stopping to wait for Doug.

"I thought we were at least on a first-name basis."

Her voice was firm. "We were, but that's in the past."

"So what's changed?"

"Look, I didn't really know you that well. I know you're a friendly guy, a nice tipper and I like you, but I make it a habit never to mix business and pleasure."

With stunned feelings Doug said the only thing that came easily to his mind. "I'm sorry for keeping you from your break, but I only wanted to make plans to see you later for a drink or something, so we could talk a bit and get better acquainted. "

"I'm sorry, Doug, but I can't do that." She smiled uncomfortably. "I hope there's no hard feelings."

Feeling rejected, Doug responded. "I had hoped for us to become friends, but that's okay. I understand...."

Before he finished, she had turned and walked away.

Doug felt bizarre and crushed.

Although they were effectively strangers, he had expected less of a cold shoulder. Sammy's odd behavior did not match the warm smiles she had traded freely a few months earlier. Gathering his bruised ego, he walked toward Jerry who was talking to a buxom brunette barmaid in a revealing outfit. As Doug approached, Jerry tossed a five-dollar bill onto her tray and she walked away.

He smiled broadly at Doug's arrival. "Did everything get worked out with your honey?"

"Not exactly! I'm not sure about what just happened."

"Come on, pal. Did you blow it with the finest babe in the whole casino? What did you say?"

"Nothing really. She said she didn't mix business and pleasure. That was basically all that happened."

"Oh, so that's what it is."

Jerry stepped closer and spoke in a softer tone.

"I think I know exactly what the problem is here. As you might guess, the casino entertains a lot of important gentlemen guests and it sometimes occurs without their wives joining them. In spite of this state's very liberal laws, the number of available women is usually a problem and we regularly ask selective employees if they want to party with discreet clients."

"Is that how she knows you?"

"Actually it is, but not in the way you would think. A couple of years ago she was invited to be on-call for involvement in those special duties."

"And you're the one who approached her."

"Yes, but it was a waste of time. She treated me exactly like she treated you a moment ago."

"I can't believe the casino tried to make her into a prostitute. What were you thinking?"

"It didn't happen that way, Doug. In this state there's already far too many hookers. After the impact of the sexual revolution began taking lives, many of our clients wanted to be with a playful woman without risking exposure to that kind of explosive history."

"What did Sammy do?"

Jerry laughed before taking another sip of his new bottle of beer. "She quit her job on the spot and left town for the next two weeks. We had a hell of a time finding her."

"So, why's she still here?"

"Too many high-rollers began asking for her. I'm sure you've noticed that her table is always full. We finally sent someone looking for her with promises that no one would ever approach her again suggesting that she participate in those kinds of duties."

"Obviously, she came back."

"Yes, but not without a big boost in pay." Jerry paused and looked briefly around the casino before focusing again on Doug. "Let me talk to her. Maybe I can fix this."

"I don't know about that. This sounds like something I can handle on my own."

"Well, I can think of one more thing that might cause her grief." Jerry winced as if there was still another big secret that he needed to divulge to Doug.

"Okay, what now?"

Doug emitted a sigh of disgust.

"You're the only person I've partied with in the past twenty years who wasn't also on the inside and working directly for papa in some questionable capacity."

"Great! That's just what I need on top of all of this. Someone else who thinks I work for the Mafia."

"Hey, pal. You do, or did you forget all about the work you do at the computer center?"

"That's not the same thing and you know it."

"Yeah, but she doesn't."

Immediately both men strolled into the spacious employee lounge to speak with Sammy. After a few tense moments she agreed to at least have breakfast with Doug in the nearby *Windjammer Cafe*.

As the limo approached the warehouse, Jerry's words brought Doug's thoughts back to the moment. "Hey there, buddy. Did you fall asleep?"

"No, just thinking about Sammy."

"Well, stop that mushy stuff. We've got to go to work for a few hours. There'll be time for that later."

The driver pulled to a stop just inside of a fenced industrial yard in front of the building. Eight-foot palleted stacks of dilapidated surplus merchandise filled the area. Weeds and litter lined the bottom of the fence on both sides. A twelve-foot wide avenue led to a wood-framed industrial building in the distance.

A small guard shack stood to their left. A single light blared rudely through one of its windows.

No one was in sight.

Jerry scanned the area before he spoke. "That's a little strange. I don't see Victor anywhere."

"Maybe he's making rounds inside of the building."

"He has no rounds. His job is to stay put in that little building." Jerry pointed to the guard shack. "If he's drunk again, I'll fire his ass on the spot."

Then he spoke to the driver. "Sal, would you please look around the yard and behind the building for him?"

"Yes, sir, Mr. Sebastino. I'll take care of that." He exited the limo and walked briskly into the darkness.

Doug and Jerry placed their beer bottles into a disposal container and stood outside of the limo.

Shadows danced across the mountains of junk and surplus items surrounding them. In the distance a small light glowed dimly above the entrance to the warehouse. They both scanned the area along side of the building.

Victor was no where in sight.

Doug's comment broke the growing silence. "This is sort of spooky. Let's get moving."

Jerry laughed as he looked at his watch. "Okay. Papa was expecting us ten minutes ago."

The men proceeded down the barren avenue.

The disrepair of the yard and building showed—aged and broken asphalt, numerous broken windows, peeled and faded paint. The abandoned look of the surroundings was done intentionally. This building housed Bruno's accounting facilities. He wanted the building to draw little attention from outsiders.

As they neared the main entrance, a crash echoed in the night air. Doug jerked and turned toward the noise. "What the hell was that?"

His eyes searched the shadows for the source.

Jerry laughed at him. "Don't be so jumpy! It was probably a scavenging animal."

"It didn't sound like that to me." Both men stopped to listen. Nothing else caught their attention.

Just out of sight and near the edge of the dilapidated building more than one pair of eyes were focused on them.

Each intruder held his breath. Too much was at stake for them to be caught before completing their mission.

Many seconds passed.

Satisfied that all was clear, Doug and Jerry walked inside and headed for the main office.

📖

Twenty minutes earlier Detective Harris had arrived at the Coleman Street warehouse with two of his men. Each brought a high-powered semi-automatic rifle with forty rounds of military style ammo.

It was not intended to be a social visit.

As Harris' car stopped at the guard shack, Victor approached. His hand rested on the handle of a well-used .38 revolver he had purchased in 1972.

The gun belt was too tight and the holster too loose.

Victor's voice betrayed his advancing age.

"You guys can't stop there. This is private property so I'll have to…."

Harris interrupted. "Hold on, Pops. We're just looking for an out of the way place to tilt a few."

Victor fanned his flashlight through the interior of the car. No guns were visible.

"Well, I don't know. That can cause me some serious trouble if you get caught here."

Harris grabbed a grocery bag from the back seat with two six packs of cold beer and pulled it onto his lap. "We weren't planning to drink all of this alone, old timer."

He ripped the bag removing a can of beer and held the frosty can in the air toward Victor.

An unforgiving thirst ravaged Victor.

His hands felt like reaching for the moist can. His mind produced images of protecting the privacy of the yard from strangers, yet his mouth was too conflicted to speak of asking the men to leave.

Harris needled him. "What's wrong, grandpa? You are going to join us for a cold one, right?"

Victor's dependency flushed over him and seized control. He held out a shaky hand.

He looked around to see if anyone else was in sight. The darkness seldom brought visitors, so it would probably be okay, he rationalized. "Sure I am."

Harris passed him the beer and asked. "Say, is there a place we can pull the car out of sight? You know, so no one will bother us for a few hours."

Struggling to open the can, Victor paused and pointed. "Let's see. How about over there behind those pallets?" He finished opening the beer and took a long drink allowing it to dribble down his chin.

He wiped it on his sleeve before taking another sip.

"Great. Once we get parked, why don't you come over for another cold one?"

Victor agreed and went into the guard shack. He set the can on a shelf out of sight.

Harris repositioned the car and began preparations for the undercover operation. After their equipment was moved closer to the warehouse, he called for Victor.

A grunt in the distance indicated he was coming for another beer. The younger men overpowered Victor, taping his hands, feet, mouth and eyes.

Once they were ready to proceed, Harris spoke to his men. "My contact swears we'll cripple the LA leadership this evening if we can take out everyone inside this piece of shit building."

Reynolds responded through a grin. "That works for me. How about you, Garcia?"

"Whatever. Just show me who I get to make dead." Officer Garcia tossed a full rifle magazine toward Reynolds. It slipped in the darkness crashing to the asphalt.

Each man froze.

Someone in the distance voiced surprise at the sound of the mishap. Harris scanned the darkness near the warehouse entrance and recognized two men, Doug Carlson and Jerry Sebastino.

He whispered. "Hey, Guys. Looks like we just hit the daily double. We'll follow those guys the rest of the way. You're on point, Reynolds."

Reynolds slung his assault rifle over his shoulder, drew his automatic pistol and clicked the safety to off.

He stood and moved cautiously toward the entrance. After several seconds Harris and Garcia did the same with their weapons and followed him.

📖

Jerry pushed on one of the doors to the main accounting office and walked inside. Bruno with two of his assistants leaned over a worktable scattered with many pages of assorted ledger paper.

For Bruno to be out this late meant that something was

seriously wrong with the business.

Coffee simmered on a hot plate in the corner. Its aroma filled the air and beckoned to their weariness.

One of the assistants wore a green plastic visor and heavy-lens wire-rimed glasses. Burly guards stood on each side of the door. Everyone looked toward Jerry and muttered a greeting. Doug followed him into the room.

"Hi, Papa. Is Victor not working tonight?"

Puzzlement filled each face, but Bruno spoke. "No. He's standing guard at the front gate, right?"

"No. I asked Sal to look for him, but nothing yet."

Bruno motioned to one of the bodyguards. "Check for him in the downstairs bathroom."

The man jumped and immediately left the room.

"What's going on, Papa? Why the late night meeting?" Jerry and Doug moved away from the double doors and closer to the crowded worktable.

An assistant stepped back to make room for them.

"It seems we've got an embezzler in Marcello's district. Someone has siphoned-off at least two million dollars during the last two months and that's more than a quarter of the usual revenue from them."

"How did you uncover this, Alan?" Jerry asked.

The accountant smiled, moved closer and explained.

"I routinely run statistical expectation tables using revenue data from all controlled districts. During the last few months it simply went crazy. When the numbers failed, I knew something was happening in district nine. Now, this type of measure doesn't tell us...."

The doors burst open with a thunderous crash.

Three large men stepped forward with automatic rifles

leveled into the small room. The working men jumped in surprise. The remaining bodyguard jerked to draw his concealed 9-mm. pistol.

Strong arms held each rifle steady then they erupted.

The bodyguard's torso ripped apart as dozens of military bullets found their mark. He flew backwards, hit the floor and slid across the room on a blanket of his own freshly spilled blood.

Bullets filled the air, pounding savagely into the walls and furniture. Bruno reached for a pistol in a nearby desk drawer. An accountant struggled to retrieve his .32 from an ankle holster.

Jerry reached for the .38 under his jacket. No one else in the room had a weapon.

Flying debris filled the air.

Alan screamed as a bullet tore into his stomach and he slipped reluctantly into the rubble.

Searing lead scrapped across Doug's forearm. He fell to his knees in pain and momentary shock.

Bruno spun to the right as two bullets planted themselves deeply inside his chest.

Jerry was ready to fire when three hi-powered bullets impacted him. He lost his forward momentum and slammed into the rear wall. Unconscious, he slid to the floor and into a growing pool of fresh blood.

From a crouched position the other accountant was now ready to shoot. He stood and fired five shots in rapid succession then he ducked back behind the desk.

Four bullets hit the wall behind Harris and his men. The last one ripped through the fabric of Reynolds' jacket. He did not respond to the near miss.

For an instant Doug's mind raced over the year of intense battle images from his Vietnam memories. Then his awareness focused on the urgency of the moment.

Time matched his concentration and slowed to meet his survival demands.

He glimpsed Bruno's gun, but it was too far away.

Intermittent bursts of gunfire competed with the sporadic rhythm of bullets expending massive energy deep inside of wood, metal and flesh.

The chaos of sound echoed throughout the building.

Broken bodies behind the desk muted its crash when overturned by the fury from a spray of high-impact bullets.

Quickly the accountant rose again above the litter and fired. His three pops were hidden among the roar of military firepower.

He drew their attention and five brass encased bullets dropped him into the flood of wreckage. Blood covered his torso and spurted randomly onto the floor. His empty eyes and distorted face of horror broadcast his lack of life.

Doug could wait no longer.

Surprised that he still survived, he sought workable options. His consciousness darted frantically around the room, quickly assessing objects and just as quickly dismissing them as useless. No weapons in sight could match the gunmen's destructive presence.

With lightning speed Doug searched his awareness.

There was only one choice. He would roll into their feet and legs prepared to disarm and fight three men at once. As a younger man, he could have done it easily.

The marines had taught him to do that and more. For now his life depended on it working one final time.

He gasped for extra air to pull the much-needed energy into his body. He felt the warmth of adrenaline surge in his veins. His heightened awareness briefly caught the sweet scent of flowing blood before being strangled by the stench of gunpowder. A death groan rose from someone fatally wounded inside the torrent of activity.

Doug was ready.

Harris had emptied his first magazine and now fumbled to replace it. Reynolds and Garcia continued firing.

The din slackened.

Debris from the room's destruction rained around Doug, but he ignored it and lunged across the floor at the feet of the men.

Harris sensed a movement and kicked blindly toward it. The massive foot caught Doug's shoulder and hurled him into the edge of a filing cabinet.

Folded metal struck his head, biting deeply into his flesh. As metal scraped across exposed bone, Doug's eyes found slumber and he rolled unconsciously to the floor on his stomach.

His blood flowed rapidly, soon encircling his head and mixing haphazardly with the life liquids of others.

From the other side of the double doors an automatic pistol erupted, delivering its full load of .38 caliber bullets into the nearly dead room.

Harris' men ducked in surprise then turned their attention to the intruder. Two dozen savage rounds spewed from the men's rifles. The door and adjoining wall collapsed from the fierce stream of bullets.

Reynolds kicked at the remnants of the shredded door. It fell away from the frame, collapsing around the fallen remains of the second bodyguard.

The firing stopped. Heavy breathing from Harris and his men was the only sound.

Quickly Reynolds and Garcia reloaded their weapons.

Harris moved forwarded prodding each of the broken bloody bodies with his foot.

None responded.

Chapter Eight

At 8:33 Tuesday morning Sammy rushed into mama's breakfast parlor. Already the women of the family gathered there, discussing the latest news and offering support to one another. Mama sat at the head of the table with Clarice on her right.

Julia sat in the next chair. Kely rose from the first seat on her left to greet Sammy.

Uncertainty filled Sammy's voice. Earlier tears had already stained her cheeks and reddened her nose.

"I hope no one else has died." She said.

For an instant Sammy's mind brushed the memories she held of Doug. His faint pleasing smile had somehow magically captured her heart during those early days. She knew from that very first moment that he was one of the truly honest men.

Usually, he gave a lot to smooth the path around him,

but he would stand and fight if pushed too hard.

Kely had told her that Doug cried very real tears when his pain became too great, but Sammy had never seen them yet. She sometimes wondered if maybe she shared hers much too easily.

She cried for days when it first dawned on her that Doug had somehow stolen into that place in her heart reserved for John and Tadpole. Finally her loss was resolved to allow them all to share that special place. Building a new life with Doug was now her most important goal.

Kely rushed into her arms.

"No, darling, no one has."

They shared a tight embrace that lingered.

After both women wiped fresh tears, Sammy took the seat next to her. Servants moved toward her, filling a plate from hot serving dishes. She raised her juice glass, sipped it slowly and looked toward mama for assurance.

Then reaching for Kely's hand, she asked. "Does anyone know what happened?"

Mama took the initiative. "Yes, child, but first how was your unexpected flight from Las Vegas?"

"It was fine, Mama. Is Doug okay?"

Feeling Sammy's anxiety Kely could not wait. "He's in good condition, dear, even walking around they say."

"Oh, good. I've been so worried about him."

With raised eyebrows mama joined back in the conversation. "Relax, my dear. It seems that he'll be fine."

Sammy could no longer hold her irritation. "Is anyone ever going to tell me what happened?"

Although mama's face would never show the pain she felt, with narrowed eyes she responded sharply.

"Certainly." Each woman turned her attention to mama as she continued. "It appears, child, that somebody tried to assassinate my son last night."

Shock flooded Sammy's face. She dropped her fork and a nearby servant rushed to assist with the mishap.

Kely touched her shoulder lightly then stroked it.

"Doug called Kely around four o'clock this morning with the news. Within thirty minutes we had all gathered here to await the latest reports from the clinic."

"So what actually happened?"

"My son was working with Jerry and Doug plus a hand full of others in their accounting offices. From out of nowhere three men assaulted them with military-styled automatic weapons and escaped unharmed. Currently two of the men are already dead. Three are listed in critical condition and one of them is my son."

Mama paused to wipe her eyes.

Tears flowed intermittently from each woman. Two servants moved quietly around the room doing their job. No eyes lingered for long on any of the grieving women.

A fresh box of tissue was placed near mama.

Sammy began to eat, but soon found that her hunger no longer required attention. After a few nibbles she pushed the steaming plate of food away.

Mama took a deep breath and continued through her sniffles. "After the assault they were all left for dead. Doug was the first to regain consciousness. He helped the others at first and then called for the doctor."

Upon hearing the mention of Doug's name Sammy's tears flowed again. She reached for a tissue.

Kely assisted her and also took another one for herself.

Mama wiped her nose before resuming.

"Jerry was shot three times and has lost a lot of blood."

A silent tear trickled down Kely's cheek.

She leaned restlessly back into her chair. Her hand again sought the comfort of Sammy.

Mama's explanation did not stop.

"He was hit in the thigh, the side and his upper arm. Luckily, they are all minor injuries. He's such a strong man I've always bragged. I know he'll recover, but he might have a bit of a limp in that one leg. My son was shot twice in the chest and one of the bullets has lodged against his spine. He's moving in and out of consciousness they say. The doctor believes he'll live through this, but...."

Mama could no longer maintain her composure. She sobbed out of control.

Sammy shifted in her seat and leaned forward.

No one else moved.

All eyes converged on Clarice. If mama could no longer speak, she would be expected to take over.

She reached for mama's hand to console her. The tears seemed to stop. Leaning over the table, she spoke softly with a strong Bronx accent. "It seems that Bruno is paralyzed up to his neck and it is not expected to improve. He will always be paralyzed."

Mama's tears erupted again.

Sammy's hand rushed to cover her mouth.

Kely reached to stroke mama's quivering arm.

A servant stopped near the head of the table between mama and Clarice. He stood in a rigid pose awaiting recognition by the lady of the house.

His eyes were focused on the door across the room.

As mama's tears flowed, Clarice spoke to the patient older servant. "Yes, Raymond?"

"Madame, the children are arriving. Shall they be visiting as usual with Mrs. Sebastino this morning?"

Mama tried to control her tears, but could not.

She just nodded then Clarice spoke again for her. "Yes, Raymond. Bring them in for a raisin muffin and juice in three minutes." Raymond acknowledged the orders, tipped his head slightly and exited in the direction of the children.

Sammy spoke up. "Excuse me, Mama, but what exactly happened to Doug?"

Mama wiped her eyes before responding. "Well, child, it seems that that man of yours was hit by a single ricocheting bullet and then somehow managed to get a nasty cut on the top of his head. They say he's in the best shape of them all, thank God."

She made the sign on the cross.

Sammy took a deep breath. "Oh, I'm so thankful for that. Will we have time to see them today?"

"Yes, child. We'll join them around ten o'clock."

In the distance the sounds of running children grew. Their shoes played an often-heard childlike rhythm on the glazed tile floor. Shouts from the girls' excitement pierced the somber moment.

The women rose, moved toward the open doors and the approaching laughter.

Mama moved to the front of the group.

Emily and Rebecca ran through the door and into the waiting arms of their great-grandmother.

📖

Harris waited for the receiver to be picked up.

A youthful voice answered. "Yeah."

"Just thought you'd like to know that the next phase has just been completed. Looks like clear sailing from here on in for you and our future business dealings."

"Good. If you've got a moment give me the details."

Harris frowned but started the story. "Last night my men and I followed them to a funky old warehouse...."

📖

Stately mature trees and well-groomed vegetation surrounded Dr. Enrico Jacobs' medical clinic. Its understated appearance broadcast his life-long commitment to a high standard of professional excellence and discretion. His Beverly Hills' clientele expected it.

Bruno demanded it.

Being Bruno's personal physician for more than thirty-three years had forged an enduring trust between the two unusual men.

Bruno and his party arrived quietly at 3:38 a.m. Four on-call doctors, all relatives of prominent local Mafia figures, had been summoned to assist with the emergency treatment. Within three hours all of the injuries had been properly attended. And fortunately no one else had died.

Doug's wounds received attention last.

Now, the sterile bandages on his head and shoulder contrasted terribly with the bloodstains on his clothing. Except for that helicopter rescue incident in Vietnam he had never seen so much of his own blood.

His battles with Mr. C were never like this. This had become an out of control blunder into full warfare inside of the Mafia. While it was not directed at him personally, he was caught right in the middle and that was way too close for comfort and personal safety.

Bruno's room held an air of death. His breathing was soft, difficult and mostly shallow. He drifted quickly and easily in and out of consciousness. He was now asleep.

The mid-morning sun bathed half the room.

Doug slept uncomfortably in a chair by the window.

Bruno stirred.

"Jerry, is that you? Come sit with me."

Doug did not hear the fatherly plea.

Again his words were soft. "Jerry, wake up!"

Yanked from his slumber Doug responded.

"What... what's wrong?"

"Oh, it's you, Doug. Where's Jerry?"

Anxiety filled his deep shaky voice.

"I'm not sure. He was just here when I sat down a while ago to rest." Doug stretched, yawned and stood.

"Is he okay? I...." Bruno raised his head slightly to look hurriedly around the room.

"He's doing real good, Bruno. He must be hobbling around somewhere. Shall I go find him?"

"No, not just yet." His head fell back to the pillow. He sighed and closed his eyes.

Listening for a breath Doug asked with a touch of panic in his voice. "Bruno, are you okay?"

"Sure. I'm fine, but I can see the end coming." His eyes remained closed as he spoke.

"Nonsense. Enrico says you're too ornery to die, especially after such a minor scuffle as this."

Bruno grinned. "That guy is such a joker."

Doug smiled and noticed Jerry walk through the door with a pair of wooden crutches. "Hey, pal. Looks like you've found a brand new set of legs."

"Yeah. Got tired of hopping around on just one leg." He skirted across the floor. "Look at this! I feel like I'm supercharged." They all laughed.

Bruno coughed for a moment.

Doug stood on one side of the bed. Jerry moved toward Bruno on the other side. Leaning his crutches in the corner he sat on the edge of the bed.

His hand reached for Bruno's forearm. "How you feeling, Papa?"

Doug pulled a chair forward and sat facing them.

Bruno said. "I must be numb all over. Except for my tongue I can't feel anything." He moistened his lips to hide the feelings of fear that came with his situation.

His eyes darted briefly to look at Doug.

"I know, Papa. You've got some pretty serious injuries." Jerry's fingers stroked Bruno's unfeeling flesh.

"What's the latest from Enrico?" Bruno knew, but had forgotten since his last nap.

"Frank and Bennie are both dead. They died immediately at the warehouse. Sergio and Michael are still in critical condition and it could go either way with them.

Victor and Sal both got only bumps on the head. They left a couple of hours ago. And Doug, well, he got hit in the head so you know he'll be all right in no time at all."

"What about you, son?" Bruno could not hide his emotion as his voice quivered. "Are you really okay?"

"Sure, Papa. I got scraped pretty bad in more than one place, but there's no lasting damage. I'm walking around almost perfectly. It just looks bad, but you know I can handle that sissy level of pain." Jerry smiled.

Bruno's eyes searched his son's face then inspected his bandages. He willed his arm, hand and fingers to reach for Jerry, but they would not move.

He closed his eyes to avoid the inactivity of his hands and arms. Momentarily he spoke. "Son, you may already know that one of those shooters was Harris."

"I know, Papa. I recognized him too."

"I must be losing my instincts. I actually met with him earlier in the day and didn't get a clue that he was planning to do such a thing." Bruno sighed.

"It's okay, Papa. Jason was never that reliable. Hey, do you think he might have hooked up with another family since you've refused to give him a job?"

Bruno pondered the thought and discarded it quickly. "No. I trust the family heads. Above all else, I have their respect. They are some of my oldest friends. They would never do a thing like this."

"But, Papa, there's a new generation coming up."

"Still, I trust them. I feel it's just Harris getting even."

Through wide eyes Doug asked. "Is that the same Jason Harris that's also an LAPD detective?"

Jerry responded. "Sure. He was on the payroll for about fifteen years. Actually he reported to Fred and took orders directly from him, so he's been off the books since you killed Fred."

"Fred? You mean Mr. C?" Doug's anxiety grew.

"Yeah. Fred recruited him back then to help protect the

casinos when the first expansions occurred."

"You mean you've got a dirty cop who for some unknown reason has turned on you? Oh boy! This shit just gets deeper and deeper." Doug stood and walked toward the door shaking his head.

"Hey buddy, what's this? You cutting out on us?"

Doug stopped at the end of the bed.

His law-abiding nature was being pushed far beyond its normal tolerance limits.

"I've been straight with the both of you from the very start. I'm not in this for the gangster routine, not any part of it. This is where I have to draw the line."

Doug turned to leave again.

"Come on, Doug. It's not that way at all."

Doug retorted. "Boy, have I heard that tune before."

Bruno spoke up to support his son.

"He's right, Doug. I've honored your every position in that respect and would never have violated a single one of your ethical requests."

Doug stopped. "How can any of this be happening? A rogue cop comes after you and almost kills us all."

"Doug, that shyster cop wanted us to give him a job. He's been after us since last year when you killed his former boss, Mr. C."

Doug hesitated to think about what was being said.

He knew they could not be held responsible for what someone else had done to them, but being in their line of business carried with it this type of personal risk.

Silently, he cursed the unusual situations that somehow made a habit of finding and complicating his life.

Then Jerry added. "And he's also the very same cop

who gave Mr. C the details about Catherine Walker's address and her very close personal connection to you."

He paused briefly then added. "Nice guy, huh?"

Doug's surprise was immediate. "Are you shitting me? That son-of-a-bitch. This same cop was also involved with Mr. C like that? How could he have done that?"

"That's how this gangster routine works, pal."

Doug paced back and forth along the end of the bed.

His anxiety flared. "Damn, I don't believe I'm stuck right in the middle of this kind of screwy bullshit again!"

"We thought you already knew all that sort of stuff about him." Jerry added cautiously.

Bruno nodded at his words.

"Not hardly. That son-of-a-bitch came to my house and played his good cop routine on me and now I find out that he knew everything about me from day one."

He even tried to cast doubt on the motives of that federal agent, Townsen and his people.

Doug swore under his breath.

Bruno's voice rose for assurance. "Doug, this is not an impossible situation. It's nothing that we can't handle, not easily, but it is fixable."

Bruno coughed several more times.

Doug raised his voice. "And just how are you going to do that? I'm stuck in the middle between a fucking crazy cop looking for cash and 90% of all the illegal activities in Los Angeles County."

Jerry and Bruno did not respond, instead they looked beyond him.

He turned to look.

Sammy stood in the open doorway. Her astonishment

at what was just said was apparent.

📖

Detective Harris had arrived at his desk early in the morning. The smell of stale coffee and lingering cigarette smoke covered everything. That had been several hours ago. Piled paperwork had chained him there.

Detective Long arrived a few minutes before ten.

"You're in early, Jason. Has anything happened?"

"Nope. Just doing some catch-up paperwork."

"It was nice getting out with you guys last night for a few drinks. How long did you and Reynolds stay at *The Watering Hole*?"

"Reynolds left twenty minutes after you did. I had one more drink before deciding to go home."

📖

With tearful reunions over and exchanged kisses dried, pain lingered on each face. Mama sat to Bruno's left. Clarice was on his right.

Each held one of his limp hands.

Bruno watched their caresses, but his wall of paralysis hid the warmth of their loving touch. His mind looked for easy explanations of what had happened.

His heart sank when none came.

Words of comfort filled the air. Impossible promises easily crowded out reason. Gradually their spirits rose. Recollections of better days soon brought laughter.

The room was now awash with smiles.

The laughter and recovery power of Bruno's family spirit filled the clinic.

Doug pulled Sammy toward the hallway.

She paused to excuse herself to the group and followed him to a nearby office.

Holding hands they stared into each other's eyes.

"Sammy, I'm so sorry this has happened. I should have anticipated something like this."

She nodded. "I know, but you had no way of knowing that any of this would happen. Have you figured out what you need to do yet?"

"No, but I can't let it get out of hand like before."

Sammy's arms encircled him. Her head rested lightly on his injured shoulder. His arms enclosed her. Secret tears flowed from her pain to mingle with his bandage.

Neither felt the real motive for the other's heartache.

Doug whispered. "Sammy, I'm so afraid this is going to be a repeat of what happened to me last year."

"That's occurred to me, too." She squeezed his chest to comfort him then sighed.

Doug's mind raced.

There must be a solution that does not involve assistance from Bruno or the mob. "I need to be smarter this time. I've already learned that getting out and away is the best way to stay alive. I need to talk to the feds before this situation goes any further."

He reached for the phone. A moment later the phone on the other end of the line rang and it was soon answered.

"LA Crime Unit, this is Agent Townsen."

"Hello, this is Doug Carlson. I'm caught in the middle of a sticky situation here and I need to speak with you off the record for a moment. Can we do that?"

"Well, Carlson, I'm not sure. Are your new playmates being naughty or just disagreeable?"

"Cut the bullshit, Townsen. I wouldn't be calling you like this unless it was something very serious."

"Okay, then tell me what's happening."

Doug paused. *There is much about this situation that needs to be left unsaid.* He chose his words carefully. "Do you know a man named Jason Harris? He's a detective working for the LAPD."

Townsen hesitated and his answer lingered. "Yes."

"I just found out he's been an informant to the mob for at least the past fifteen years. Did you know that?"

"Carlson, don't feed me a line of bull like that. If true, this is a very serious charge you're making. I'm not willing to buy it unless you've got some pretty substantial evidence to prove it in a court of law."

"Well, I've got zip for the moment, but I know for sure that it's true. You'll just have to take my word about it until I can prove it later."

"And what does that mean? Will you be coming up with some hard evidence then?"

"I can't really say, just yet. Something very big is happening and I'm stuck right in the middle of it. Exactly the last place I want to be ever again."

"Mr. Carlson, can you excuse me for a moment?"

"Sure."

Doug placed his hand on the mouthpiece and whispered to Sammy. "He's got me on hold for a moment."

Awareness of what was happening stunned Sammy's face. She grabbed the phone and raised her voice. "Doug, hang it up! He's tracing your call. He's trying to find our location right now."

Doug resisted.

Their arms fell away from the hugs.

"Hang it up, God-damn it." She pressed the disconnect button and the phone went dead.

"Why did you do that? That's one of the few people I still trust to help me."

"Maybe so, but for now the situation is way too messy and out of control. I don't trust anyone."

"Come on, Sammy! We're stuck right in the middle of a very deadly predicament. I'd like to know there's a friendly face somewhere out there if we need help."

"Me too, but I believe Bruno when he says you're involvement is purely accidental. I'd like to give him and Jerry a chance to fix it if they can. What do you say, hon?"

Doug stepped away and turned his back to her.

His hand rubbed across his face then to the back of his head trying to sort the details. That first angry encounter with Mr. C flooded his awareness. Doug had won the war, but lost a very important battle.

He was unwilling to ever face that possibility again. There must be another way he thought. His conflicted mind swirled with unworkable options.

Sammy approached from the rear.

Her arms encircled him.

Her face pressed hard into his back. She mouthed the words *I love you* and squeezed him.

Doug felt the warmth of her breath and turned to face her. "Sammy, I'm afraid to admit it, but I don't know what else to do."

"It's okay, hon, neither do I. Let's rejoin the others."
Doug nodded and they left the office.

📖

An agent walked hurriedly into Townsen's office.
"Sir, you sent for me?" The man asked.
"Agent Wilson, do you remember Doug Carlson? He was involved in that shoot-out with some of Sebastino's people late last year."
Wilson nodded. "Yes sir, I do."
"Something's come up with him and I'm not exactly sure of how to read it."
Wilson nodded again and Townsen continued.
"When you were in direct contact with him last year, would you have taken his word at face value?"
There was another nod. "That's pretty close to what I was thinking about him, too."

📖

Back in Bruno's room the sickroom festivity continued. The granddaughters had finally been allowed to join the group. They each sat on the end of Bruno's bed.
Witches, bears and flying horses were the new topics being discussed. Kely's pretense of being a witch caused the girls to recoil in feigned horror then burst into a bout of uncontrollable giggles.
As Sammy and Doug reentered the room, Jerry whispered to them. "You two all right?"
Sammy smiled and Doug nodded.

They closed the door and sat at the end of the bed.

Jerry touched Doug's bandaged forearm and asked softly. "How's it feeling?"

"Not too bad. Really nothing more than a scrape."

Bruno's voice spoke softly. "Emily, Rebecca, can I ask the pooh bears to take your mom for a walk to see some of the interesting things around the hospital?"

Emily responded again for the two of them. "Sure, Papa. Is it her first time visiting here? Is there anything special she wants to see?" Rebecca climbed excitedly from the bed with mama's gentle assistance.

Smiling Bruno added. "I'm sure she'll have questions as you give her your special tour."

"I can do that, Papa. Come on, Beck." They ran toward the door. Julia smiled knowingly at her papa and followed the girls out of the room.

When the door was again closed, Bruno spoke.

"Ladies and gentlemen, we need to put our heads together and find a solution to this painful dilemma."

A number of heads nodded.

Resigned, yet determined smiles covered all faces.

Jerry spoke. "Getting even with Harris will be easy, but the heat from downtown will be god-awful intense."

"If we talk of these things, son, I'll have to ask the women to leave and probably you too, Doug."

Mama rose to leave the room, but Kely prompted her to retake her seat, then Kely nudged Jerry to act.

He raised his hands to make the signs of a surrender. "Okay, okay, I'll say it."

"Is there something you need to say to me, son?"

"Yes, Papa, there is."

Through raised eyebrows Bruno inquired. "And this involves allowing our women to participate in, and know, the unsightly details of our business."

"Yes, Papa, it does." He paused.

Speaking such words to his father was very difficult.

"Well…." Bruno prodded him.

Kely nudged him again and after inhaling a deep breath Jerry finally responded. "Papa, we've talked of this matter before, but now is a perfect time for us to finally take the necessary action to implement it."

"Are we talking about a totally new direction for the family business?" Bruno aided his uncomfortable son.

"Yes, Papa. Now is probably the right time for us to consider making such changes. We can remove these unacceptable risks from our new family members. The way things have been in the past, death finds us way too easily. Papa, we have more money than we'll ever be able to spend in a hundred lifetimes. Can we now at least consider such options?"

Kely smiled and held her breath. Anticipation grew on each face. Doug secretly praised Jerry for his timing. He knew that this would be a tough sell.

Bruno hesitated to contemplate the request from one of the few people he would allow to speak of it.

Silence shouted the seconds as they passed.

Finally Bruno spoke. "Let's see if I understand this. You are asking me to retire and relinquish all of my control over the family business. Is that it?"

Sammy and Kely nodded.

Jerry nodded too. "In a sense that's it, Papa."

"That's too much to ask of me under the circumstances

even from you, son, but I'll consider disengaging from everything over the next year or so." Sammy and Kely smiled and spontaneously hugged their men.

Bruno continued.

"Now that we have that settled can we move on to dealing with the current problem?"

Everyone nodded.

Jerry moved closer.

Bruno continued. "For the safety of everyone involved, Jerry, I want you to call the airport. Have Harold prepare the plane. We'll leave early this afternoon for *The Desert Phoenix*. A few of weeks of extended relaxation in Cabo should clear everyone's head."

A new excitement gripped the women.

Sammy and Kely rushed to assist mama. They left the room immediately to find Julia. Many preparations for such a trip needed to be made.

"Are you sure, Papa?"

"Yes. What was that you called it, Doug, R&R?"

"Yes sir, that's it, rest and relaxation."

"Are you okay with this, Doug?"

"I think it's a very smart move, Bruno. We can all use the recovery time to sort out our feelings. And, the security will be much easier to maintain there."

"What about you, son?" Bruno asked.

With a deeply concerned look on his face Jerry quizzed his father. "Papa, we're not running away, are we?"

Pausing to consider his response, Bruno answered firmly. "No, we're going to a safe place to heal and make plans to really get Harris for what he's done."

Chapter Nine

Harris' phone rang. He brushed a stack of reports as he reached for it. They toppled onto his work. He swore before getting the receiver positioned on his ear.

"Harris."

The caller explained in a troubled rush. "They're gone. Somebody has taken those god-damn bodies."

"Hold on, Reynolds. What the hell are you trying to say? Slow it down a bit."

Reynolds took a deep breath then continued.

"A while ago I asked a friend in patrol to cruise the warehouse saying I had a tip about shots being fired there last night. She spent fifteen minutes scoping out the area and swears the place is totally deserted. And get this—I couldn't believe my ears. There were no bodies and she didn't see a single drop of blood anywhere. I don't like it! Something is very wrong with this picture."

Harris tried to console him.

"Take it easy. We aren't dealing with just any punk-ass street pushers here. These guys have a high-class organization. They are...."

"I still don't like it. They're supposed to be dead."

"Reynolds, stop acting like this. It's not the end of the world. There's a perfectly logical explanation for what's happened. I'll make some phone calls to see what's happening. You finish your shift and stay calm. I'll catch up with you at *The Hole* later this afternoon."

They said goodbye and hung up the phones.

Ten minutes later Harris fabricated a reason to leave his office. He went straight to the police parking lot where he phoned his inside contact on the cell phone.

The seconds dragged until the phone was answered.

"Yeah."

Harris tried to sound calm, but felt he was not. "It looks like someone is playing games with those bodies."

"I was hoping you'd call, Jason. It seems that what you say happened, didn't. Can you explain that?"

"Well, sir. I just learned about it myself and I'm baffled by what I've heard."

"Did you finish the next phase of our plan or not?"

Harris did not like the uncomfortable feeling he had. "Yes, but I can't explain the disappearance of the bodies."

"This does not look good, Jason. Get back to me after you find them."

He hung up the receiver.

📖

The final leg of the eighty-minute drive to the Long

Beach Airport was done in six rented vans. The ultimate scope of the plot against Bruno was unknown and he was taking no chances with the family involved and in the open like this. They left their limousines in a Culver City parking garage. Belongings and family members were transferred quickly. Seven-armed bodyguards escorted them in three other nondescript vehicles.

The entourage pulled adjacent to the company jet at 3:25 p.m. Ten minutes later they were airborne.

Bruno had been sedated and was comfortably strapped into a fully reclined window seat over the wing. At his side mama held his limp hand.

Clarice was seated two rows away and Dr. Jacobs sat nearby. Two nurses arrived at the last moment.

Doug and Sammy took seats in the rear of the plane near the galley, bar and restroom. Julia and the kids claimed the entire first row in the plane. Kely and Jerry sat in the same row with Bruno and mama. The bodyguards, a hand full of servants and Bruno's drivers filled half of the remaining seats.

Kely leaned to mama and whispered. "How's papa?"

"He's resting, dear."

Mama smiled and closed her eyes.

Kely returned mama's warm smile then sat upright in her seat. Her head turned toward Jerry.

He was already asleep, so she closed her eyes.

📖

The Watering Hole was a dive. When its police patronage increased two years earlier, its status did not. Fast food, brew and safety were its primary attractions. The LAPD day shift ended at 3:30 p.m.

Officers in civvies began arriving ten minutes later.

Garcia and Reynolds had claimed the booth in the corner shortly after their shifts had ended. Their table was dark and private so they could talk without being overheard. Both men had finished their third drink before Harris arrived.

Motioning to the overflow of glasses sitting on the table Harris criticized them. "What's this pile of garbage? It looks like a couple of god-damn lushes are sitting here." Reynolds waved to get the attention of a bar hostess.

Garcia's upset filled the booth.

"Jason, hitting Sebastino last night was a stupid fucking move." He slid across the padded bench making room for Harris to sit next to him. "I should have never listened to those grandiose plans of yours."

Harris frowned at him.

The hostess arrived.

Harris grinned at the buxom brunette as she spoke. "What'll y'all have?" The dainty outfit she wore barely covered her shoulders, cleavage and thighs.

Garcia spoke, motioning toward himself and Reynolds. "We'll have more of the same."

He tossed a twenty toward her on the table.

As the young woman began clearing the table, Harris ordered for himself. "I'll have whisky over and tell Pete not to use that cheap shit." He straightened his tie. She wiped the table with a moist towel. Before she left Harris added. "Better yet, make that a double."

She left and walked toward the bar.

Reynolds spoke to Harris. "Did you ever find out what happened to those bodies?"

Harris shook his head.

"Not exactly. Seems like nothing at all has happened. Nobody on the street knows anything about anything. Is anyone surprised at that?"

"Or maybe they just won't tell you." Garcia chided.

"Back off, Mister! I don't need any more grief on this from you. I called my contact in one of the families and he says they can't find them either."

Harris' eyes narrowed.

Garcia turned to Reynolds who responded to Harris.

"I think he's right. We really fucked this up royally. If anyone ever finds out that we were involved in this, we're all dead, totally and completely fucking dead."

Leaning back Harris breathed a sigh of exasperation. "Come on, guys. We're the ones with the badges. They may be wealthy, but they're still low-life scumbags."

Reynolds was not pleased. "That kind of trash talk is not helping me feel better about this. Something's wrong and you don't seem to have a clue about it. Just answer me this one thing—where are those bodies?"

Harris was defiant. "Don't know. Don't give a shit."

Garcia could not control himself. "And why is that?"

"We pumped more than enough lead into those guys last night so that none of them could have survived it. So what if someone came along and cleaned it up. They're all still very dead, right?"

Reynolds and Garcia both shook their heads in disbelief. Harris was unaffected by their concern.

Garcia added. "Yeah, but why the secrecy? That's exactly what's got me so much on edge."

Reynolds nodded his concern.

"That's probably the only way for the higher-ups to keep a lid on a big turf war." Harris laughed. "Haven't you guys ever seen that kind of stuff in the movies?"

📖

By 3:45 four servants had assumed the role of steward-esses and refreshments had been dispensed. A lite meal was now being served. Several people sat at the bar. Most of the others remained in their seats. The two girls played in the wide aisle. Julia alternated between watching them and taking quick naps.

Bruno had been awake several times. He was in good spirits, but had also suffered two long nearly uncontrolla-ble coughing spells. A few sips of cool ginger ale helped him to breathe a bit easier and to then get back to sleep.

After mama finished her meal she again reached for his hand. With her seat partially reclined she turned toward him and spoke to him as though he were still her little boy of many years ago.

Jerry yawned, took a deep breath and stretched.

Restful sleep on an airplane was tough to get, he thought. He was awake now. Kely's head rested lightly against his shoulder.

Short brown sculpted locks framed her face.

She seemed to be sleeping much better than he was. He moved slightly. She shifted a little and without waking her head turned slowly away from him.

The sun sank low in the distance.

Jerry lowered the shade on the window. Now the waning sun would not shine directly in her face.

Mama's eyes were closed.

Bruno slept quietly.

Jerry stood, moved cautiously past Kely and searched for Doug. A soft hand found his.

"You feeling restless, dear?" Mama whispered and then gazed up at him.

"I think so. Sleeping like this in the middle of the day just doesn't seem respectable to me."

"I know, but I'll be awake until your papa is feeling better. If I can sleep now, I'll feel much better later."

She closed her eyes to return to her nap.

"It's okay, Mama. You get some more rest."

📖

Alcohol now controlled the judgment of each man at the table. Harris' confidence could not be shaken. Garcia's concern deepened by the hour. Reynolds was sure a mob hit was being planned against them at that very moment.

With an overflowing mug of beer in his hand Sergeant Patterson approached their table.

It was 4:05 p.m.

Few empty seats remained.

By now all were feeling happy.

"How the hell you doing, Reynolds?" Patterson slid into the seat next to him.

Reynolds retreated just enough to avoid being embarrassed by the closeness of another man. His mood changed. "I'm good. Where you been keeping yourself,

Ron?" Two partial pitchers of beer sat on the table.

Garcia reached for one and filled Patterson's mug after his first gulp drained half of it.

"My wife's redoing the kitchen and it seems like I'm doing all of the damn work."

The men laughed.

"She started early in the summer, replacing appliances. Now, it has to have new paint, cabinets and counters."

Harris spoke. "My wife did that a few years ago too. She was on me so much to get it done on her schedule that I finally hired someone to do it."

Patterson grinned. "I hadn't thought of that."

Several chuckled.

He raised his mug as if making a toast.

They all took a big drink. Garcia topped off their mugs. The hostess retrieved the empty pitchers.

Harris nodded for a refill.

Reynolds fixation on the woman's curvaceous body was obvious as she walked away.

Patterson nudged him. "You still dating Celeste?"

Reynolds smiled as if to brag. "Yeah, I've got to get my mind off of her after the antics she put on last night."

📖

Sammy read. Doug slept. Jerry approached them.

She saw him, looked up and smiled.

He grinned then leaned on the seat in front of her.

She turned the book over on her lap.

Jerry spoke. "You must hate flying on this plane by now. Making that trip twice a week for months would drive me crazy."

She closed her book, smiled and shook her head.

Jerry continued. "Did you ever get that new apartment you were talking about?"

"No. I felt like I needed to move, but it would have been too much trouble, a lot more than I wanted to deal with at the time."

Jerry nodded and she finished her comment.

"So I decided to put it off a while in favor of something more permanent."

Jerry's eyes widened. "Oh!"

Sammy shook her head. "You guys, you always get the wrong idea on everything."

📖

Townsen's phone rang.

He laid his engraved pen on top of a file folder labeled SECRET and grabbed for the phone. He leaned back in his chair and stretched out his long legs.

"Hello, Agent Townsen."

"It's me, sir. I've looked everywhere for Carlson this afternoon. He's gone, just vanished!"

"What's that mean?"

"He was last seen at work on Monday afternoon. In the past twenty-four hours there's been no sign of him at all. No one's seen or talked to him today and he failed to show up for work this morning."

"Strange. I just talked to him a few hours ago."

"Is there a problem, sir?"

"I'm not sure." Townsen pushed his chair away from the table. He turned toward the wall as he thought more about Carlson's words. He crossed his legs.

The caller inquired. "Sir?"

"There's a detective with LAPD named Harris. Pull everything about him that you can get your hands on."

📖

Sammy went back to her book after Doug awakened.

He and Jerry began their bantering ritual. After several minutes Sammy was bothered. "Come on, guys. Move it to the bar so I can read in peace."

They moved without objection.

At the bar they kept an empty stool positioned between them, then they turned to face each other. A fridge to one side held their brew. A microwave on the other side had just finished a batch of popcorn for the kids.

They would get the next batch for munching.

Jerry took a drink of beer and spoke. "What do you remember about the shooting?"

"Nothing unusual, just the quickness with which it all happened. My eyes were always on that guy in the middle. What about you?"

"I was out of it so quick. I only remember the first few rounds being fired and that's all. Bingo and I was down."

"Did you see Bennie using that .32 caliber pistol he carries in his sock?"

"No. Did he fire it before they nailed him?"

"Damn straight. He fired it at least five or six times at them. That mousy guy sure did show some balls."

"Good. I always liked him. Did you know he was in the army in Vietnam?"

"You're shitting me, where?"

"You know, I can't remember the name of the base now. Somewhere around Saigon is all I recall."

"Was he a bean counter even then?"

"Probably."

A servant placed a fresh bowl of popcorn on the bar in front of the two men. Doug reached for another beer then noticed that Sammy had reclined her seat and appeared to be sleeping.

After his brief distraction Doug restarted the conversation. "How many times has it been now?"

Jerry looked puzzled.

"You know, bullet holes. How many times have you ever been shot?" Doug explained.

Jerry shook his head and smiled.

"In Vietnam I spent two years riding shotgun in the door of an attack helicopter shooting at everything that moved and never got a single scratch. In the last year I've been plugged six times in Los Angeles. Go figure."

Doug aimed his fist at Jerry's uninjured shoulder and planted a light friendly punch. "It must be the type of life you've led, buddy."

"Okay, *mud marine*, what about you?"

"Except for a bunch of minor nicks and scrapes just once." Doug hesitated, wishing that he had said nothing.

Jerry needled him. "Come on, pal. You can tell me, it's just one jarhead to another."

"*The Nam* only got me one time and I ain't talking about it." Again Doug hesitated.

He knew it was no big deal, but he had not mentioned it to anyone since it had happened.

"It can't be much of an injury. It didn't affect your behavior in that big row you had with Mr. C last year."

"It's a bit embarrassing. Let's just leave it at that."

Jerry's memory was jogged.

"Okay, but that reminds me of a situation like that in *Nam* with some poor fucking grunt. I think his unit was on a search and destroy mission that took them halfway to hell and gone. Those *ground pounders* had been in the area for a few days. I think he was in the Seventh Marines. A lucky sounding name, but not that day."

Doug nodded.

He had been assigned to the seventh at the end of his tour and he remembered there was one time they got suckered into a major butt kicking.

Jerry continued his story.

"Most of the day I had flown armed-escort for medivac choppers to pick up the wounded. It had been a very long and busy day. I heard those marines had taken fifty percent casualties before noon on that last day."

Doug nodded because it sounded like his platoon.

"Around two o'clock the last fifty of those fighting motherfuckers were being extracted from the *landing zone*. I remember watching it all from the air.

"By then they had been fully surrounded and their perimeter was being forced smaller by the minute, but those jarheads just wouldn't give up. This was the classic fighting withdrawal. I thought it was absolutely beautiful. The discipline those *mud marines* displayed was to be envied.

"As they pulled back toward the chopper their contact with the enemy remained intense and of course very deadly. A handful of marines had already discarded their weapons to drag their wounded and dead comrades to the choppers. I watched the aircrew scrambling like hell on the ground to load them all.

"There was barely enough room to land a CH-46, but one was on the ground and another waited overhead for the final extraction. With barely enough marines left on the ground to maintain control of the *LZ*, the first chopper rose with its bloody cargo.

"The second one descended immediately into the fray and was hit from all sides with incoming small arms fire. I knew every marine on that flight crew and they all died in that *LZ* except for the copilot.

"My Huey had already fired all of its rockets and the M-60 ammo was getting low, but we maintained cover fire for the marines still on the ground. A horrible deadly frightening moment, but one I'll never forget.

"Suddenly there was a maddening scramble for the chopper, but three of those marines held their ground, providing a final line of resistance for the *LZ*. Once on-board a number of them opened fire from the windows of the chopper to support their buddies still on the ground. I could imagine hearing some of them yelling like crazy for the others to hurry and get aboard.

"One marine stood just outside the hatch, firing an M-16 from this shoulder. When it was empty he tossed it aside and picked up another one lying nearby. That must have been when the pilot was killed because the chopper started rising. At the last second he jumped toward the door and several others pulled him inside.

"I yelled over the intercom—there's men still on the ground. The pilot responded—I see'em. Hang on, we're going in. The Huey jerked and dived.

"We settled about four feet off the ground near a mound. We rotated slowly so the M-60's could spray the entire area with bullets. Those marines moved closer while still maintaining their fire. As one of them went down, the second marine moved to assist him. The firing continued from all sides of the *LZ*. As they got closer to the chopper, the third one went down.

"The pilot sat the Huey on top of the mound. A strange combination of gun grease and high explosives filled the air. I will never forget that unusual smell.

"The gunner on the other side of the chopper had been hit, but continued firing. The three marines were now on my side. Finally, that uninjured marine tossed his weapon and assisted both of his injured buddies as they moved toward me. I fired over their heads at the advancing enemy.

"He aided one to walk and dragged the other by an arm. Bullets peppered the ground around them, as they inched closer to the Huey. I was sure I saw the man being dragged get hit again and go limp, but his lifesaving grasp from the other marine was not released.

"As they reached the side of helicopter, the first marine hobbled aboard. The uninjured marine turned to load the limp one. I knew the man was dead when I saw that half his face and head were shot away.

"I yelled to the pilot—Got'em! Suddenly the chopper rose quickly. I grabbed for the remaining marine and pulled him toward the door. His feet dangled briefly until they found one of the runners below the *chopper*.

"Then almost like a final insult from those pursuing Viet Cong soldiers that brave marine took the final bullet in the backside. It hit him squarely in the butt and splattered his blood all over me."

Doug's mouth flew open.

"I pulled him inside and on top of his dead buddy. That *mud marine* grimaced, but never once uttered a single word of pain during the whole flight. He...."

Tears streamed down Doug's cheeks. "How the hell did you know about that?" He begged.

Doug wiped his face. He could barely speak. "That was me. That *mud marine* was me." He kept nodding as if his words were not being heard.

"You're shitting me, right?" Jerry acknowledged.

Doug shook his head.

Jerry's surprise was apparent, but he continued.

"Don't do this, Doug. Don't fuck with me on something as important as this is to me. I've always wondered about that crazy fucking jarhead."

Finally it sunk in.

"I'll be god-damn. He was to become my best friend in the whole damn world."

Chapter Ten

Harris watched Patterson stagger away and could hold his anger no longer. "Reynolds, you are one sorry-ass shit-for-brains loser. What the fuck was all that bullshit you laid on him about Celeste? Can't you just keep your fucking trap shut?"

"What the hell is wrong with you?" He yelled back.

"Patterson may be drunk, but he knows you're feeding him a line of bullshit. All those lame comments about your girlfriend and how you're not getting laid. If he figures any of this out, I'll personally bury your wisecracking ass."

📖

The airport at Los Cabos was now barely twenty minutes away. The sun readied for its daily exit. Shadows darkened in the sand, sagebrush and water below the high-flying jet. The lingering warmth of the tropical night air was not yet apparent.

Sammy and Kely rested in soft chairs in the lounge area. Nearby Doug and Jerry still maintained their drinking positions at the bar. Awakened recently Bruno and mama spoke softly of what had been.

Bruno coughed occasionally. The girls cuddled warmly against their mother. All three slept soundly.

Dr. Jacobs neared the bar heading for the bathroom.

Jerry spoke to him as he passed. "Enrico, is papa really going to be okay?"

The aged physician paused to ponder Bruno's injuries. His decades of experience had regularly failed to provide the proper response in situations like this. "He seems to be, son, but that cough is starting to worry me. There's a very big risk in moving someone with his particular injuries. I'll feel a lot better when he's finally resting safely in his own bed."

"Me, too."

"It won't be much longer now." Enrico continued.

Sammy and Kely stood to approach the bar. They had observed the earlier emotional moments between their men. Things seemed somewhat normal again.

Kely spoke. "What are you guys doing?"

Jerry smiled reaching for her. "Just passing the time. You beautiful babes planning to join us?"

Neither of them responded to his male comment.

Sammy moved to Doug and placed her arm across his shoulders. He leaned into her arms and they exchanged a quick kiss. With a brief wink Doug added.

"I guess we'd better stop talking about old girlfriends

for a while." He smiled.

The women ignored his comment, too.

Sammy kissed Doug on the ear.

Kely shook her head.

"Don't you guys ever talk about anything except women, sports and being in the Marines?"

Both shook their heads.

The pilot announced that all passengers should reclaim their seats for landing. It was 5:53 p.m.

The sound of the engines changed and grew louder.

📖

Garcia spoke to Harris. "I'm full of brew and low on chew. You guys about ready to get some dinner?"

Harris nodded and started to slide across the bench. He had been hungry for sometime, but seldom mentioned eating when he was drinking.

Through a good-sized buzz, Reynolds slurred. "Fellows, I have just one thing to say before we go."

He sat up straight like he was preparing to deliver a long-practiced speech.

Everyone paused for him.

His slur was quite obvious. "Not another word from me about any of this shit."

📖

Bruno's transfer to the waiting van went smoothly.

Enrico, Clarice and mama stayed by his side for the drive to *The Desert Phoenix* hacienda. Everyone else filled two stretch limos and a taxi to capacity.

The late-afternoon warmth of Lower Baja brushed the growing darkness. A light breeze occasionally tossed the stillness. Lights pierced the distance.

Dusk would become night in minutes.

First, the smooth, seldom-traveled road took them to the south and then west. Fifty-five minutes later they turned into the stately grounds of Bruno's winter estate. The scent of the nearby ocean lingered in the air. Darkness had replaced the shadows.

The servants hustled to clear the vehicles with the aid of the year-round caretaker staff. Bruno was carried to the master's suite. The family members and guests were shown to their rooms.

The grandeur of the building and furnishings was not lacking. There was much less in the way of carpeting, tapestries and finely woven rugs and much more in decorative tile, marble and expensive stonework than in the family estate in Beverly Hills. Elegant archways, sparkling fountains and desert greenery adorned many spaces.

The main veranda overlooked the roaring surf a hundred feet below. The ocean was seldom quiet.

In an hour and a half all had finished their dinner and began converging in Bruno's room. A massive canopy bed filled one wall. Shades of brown, green and blue pleased their tired eyes. Comfortably positioned on the bed, Bruno's smile pleased the heart, but knowledge of his predicament shattered it.

An ocean breeze toyed with thin curtains hanging on an open balcony window. Its faint coolness could not match the lingering heat.

The girls stood next to the bed saying their prayers for papa. Julia lifted each of the girls to deliver a goodnight kiss to him. After a moment she prompted them to follow her to their nearby bedroom.

Bruno smiled as they exited the room.

Mama moved closer to comfort him. For a moment the room was quiet.

Bruno's voice was soft and noticeably shaky. "Is everyone here?" His eyes darted among the faces. Several muttered yes. Carlos left the room to summon the rest of the household servants.

Shortly Julia returned with a worried smile.

Bruno continued.

"Enrico tells me that time is probably short." Gasps filled the quiet room. Mama shifted uncomfortably in her chair. Her grip tightened on Bruno's stony fingers.

Someone sniffled.

"Now that my family is finally safe, we must make plans for dealing with our situation tomorrow."

Jerry rose and cautioned. "Papa, we should talk about all of this in the morning when you're feeling rested."

Bruno's voice cracked. "I'm afraid...."

Jerry reacted to the potential loss. "No, Papa. It's okay. You'll be fine."

Doug reached to touch his arm then whispered. "Come on, buddy. Since we can't change it just let it happen."

Kely reached for Jerry's other arm.

Together they guided him back into his seat.

Through a forced painful smile Bruno continued.

"During the past few months I've learned that none of you wish to have any involvement in the family business.

Quite a surprise for an old man at a time like this, but never the less I love you all and have allowed for that. I've decided to make a number of other arrangements."

Sammy and Kely's faces both held grim smiles, believing that Bruno spoke these final words directly to them. Now their men could have safer jobs that would not bring them so much worry.

"I've directed my friend Jay Feldman to handle everything that's necessary. He'll sever all ties with the company businesses. Then my personal assets and family real estate will be put into trusts that he says will generate a substantial income stream for my family."

Tears began to flow around the room.

Bruno coughed briefly.

"Son, will you administer those trusts for me and dispense the cash as I would have done?"

Jerry fought his tears and lost. "Yes, Papa."

"First, mama will be taken care of. She says she might like to travel some if she's able. I want her to do that. Then, you'll take care of the grandchildren, including any new ones, with college costs." Jerry nodded.

Bruno coughed again and Enrico moved quickly to comfort him. They exchanged brief whispers and the doctor took a seat next to the bed.

Mama wiped Bruno's mouth before he spoke again.

"There are more personal wishes, but they are detailed in the documents Jay prepared for me so I won't recount them any further considering the circumstances.

"A father's dream is to produce a living legacy for those who follow. Tonight I am pleased to have capable, accomplished and determined men and women around me.

Your strength of mind fills me with personal satisfaction. Your growing love for each other lightens and pleases my heart. All of you, my dear ones are my legacy. I can now die a proud and very happy man."

Sobs and sniffles erupted around the room.

Bruno coughed but now with less energy.

Enrico tended him.

Several held their breath for signs that he was okay.

With a stethoscope to Bruno's chest he shook his head. Enrico leaned forward and whispered to mama.

"It's near. He probably won't speak again."

Mama stood and motioned for all to gather around. "It's time to say goodbye to papa."

Chapter Eleven

Sadness filled the early morning hours at *The Desert Phoenix*. Bruno's passing at 1:03 a.m. brought hours of wailing from mama and Clarice. Tears flowed freely from family, friends and servants alike.

Sorrow held many hearts and reddened many eyes.

At sunrise it stopped.

Now most were making time for extra sleep.

The day's heat grew quickly. The ocean breeze was not nearly cool enough. This would be a scorching day.

📖

Agent Wilson entered Townsen's open office door at 9:05 a.m. "Excuse me, sir, but I have the reports on Detective Harris that you requested yesterday."

He laid them on the table and stood at attention.

Townsen slowly opened the top folder and began reading. "Let's see... Jason Robert Harris... hmmm... how much of this stuff have you read, Wilson?"

He responded. "All of it, sir."

"This guy's a real Boy Scout, isn't he?"

"Yes, sir."

"Carlson says this cop takes money from Sebastino and the Mafia. What do you think?"

"Tough call sir. In a dead heat, I'd pick Carlson."

📖

The last family member walked into the dining room at 11:43 a.m. for lunch. Bruno's place at the head of the table was set as though he would take it at any moment. Reddened eyes around the table gave testament to the fact that he would not.

Seats prepared for two of his closest friends who had just arrived from Los Angeles flanked it. His most trusted bodyguards had taken the next few chairs. Carlos, the chauffeurs and all servants of more then twenty-five years were seated next. Mama sat at the other end of the table with the family and the closest friends of the neighbors who lived nearby.

This meal was prepared to be shared by those Bruno had loved and depended upon so faithfully through the years. It began in silence.

After each small portion of food arrived the next person in turn was expected to briefly stand and speak of any special situation or circumstance that had occurred between him and the dearly departed.

Each person regardless of job or status would use his given name today.

Sweet figs arrived.

Bruno's life-long associate, friend and personal attorney, Jay Feldman, stood.

He wiped his eyes and began.

"Life may be long or short, but sadly it is never enough when spirits like Bruno fill and caress our heart. His generosity, kindness and compassion touched many of those he knew. His devoted life makes me proud that I was able to be made a part of it."

The next course would be garden fresh peas.

📖

Reynolds beeper activated.

He recognized Harris' number and began looking for a public phone. Within minutes Harris' phone rang.

"Harris."

"This is Reynolds."

"You feeling better?"

"Not much better. Next time I drink like that will you please just shoot me while I'm drunk and passed out? This headache is torture."

Harris chuckled. "Don't tempt me."

Reynolds spoke with barely a smile. "What's up?"

"There's no word on Sebastino. You heard anything?"

"No, not a thing."

"I wonder what's behind all of this?"

"Shall I ask around?" Reynolds queried.

"No. Just sit on it for now. Boy, I sure don't understand any of this. We pop the biggest underworld target on the West Coast and it's turned into a nonevent."

📖

The twenty-third course arrived—lavender rice pudding, Doug stood to praise a man of paradox.

He smiled at mama, then looked at Jerry.

"Bruno, I'm sorry to say, is somewhat of a recent friend, but one unlike few others I've ever had. His presence in a room seized everyone's attention, although this enormous power of his was quite easily overshadowed by his heightened concern for family and friends. In the beginning I experienced intense conflict at getting too close to him, but his vitality, forcefulness and unusual softness produced such a divergent set of personal images for me that I could not resist his charm.

"Today I'm saddened by the lack of time we shared. The loss of such a man impoverishes each person who knew and loved him, as well as those who will never know his generosity. I will miss him." He attempted to force a smile through pursed lips and sat.

The twenty-fourth course arrived—caramel pistachio pudding. Jerry rose to honor his father.

"I'm very pleased that papa was so well loved. Your participation in this memorial for him is very special. I'm deeply moved by the stories I've heard. This will not be an easy day for me."

Tears stole onto his cheeks and he blotted them with his well-used handkerchief.

"I'm impressed that the actions and needs of others are

now brought so sharply into focus for me. I realize how they have all helped make my life what it has become. To all of you, my very dear friends, I reaffirm—if my father treated you like family, in the future so shall I." Emotions welled on his face and he wiped moist eyes as he sat.

The twenty-fifth course was rum-raisin pudding.

Mama prepared to speak. She remained in her seat.

"Ladies and gentlemen, your loving tribute to my son, Bruno, this morning is indeed a special time for me. May each of your lives be filled with the same family pleasures you've shared with us."

The final course consisted of a single sliver of rich dark chocolate. This small dish was placed only for Bruno.

Sadly, it would not be eaten.

📖

Harris arrived before 3:00 p.m. This was unusual for him since he seldom kept to a schedule, but this meeting was different from most. Before Townsen made his arrival additional planning was needed.

Reynolds was hidden in nearby shrubbery in case there was trouble that could not be resolved on the spot. The location was wooded and secluded. That was exactly how they had planned it.

Townsen's car approached and pulled to a stop several feet away. He rose from the driver's seat and spoke before he closed the door.

"Harris, I'm hearing some very bad reports about you. You got anything to say for yourself?"

"Nope. I came here to listen, remember?"

"Okay, I'll get right to the point. Do you know where Doug Carlson is?"

"How the hell should I know anything about him?"

"Don't even try to work that stuff with me, Harris. I already know that you and your boys are gunning for some of Sebastino's people. Is Carlson's disappearance another of those incredibly stupid moves?"

"Townsen, you're pathetic! This is some weird shit you're putting out. Someone takes out a big-time local Mafia crook and you get all touchy-feelie for him. Exactly what kind of a law enforcement officer are you?"

"Just answer the question. Where is Carlson? I think you know something and I want to hear it, now."

"Sorry, Red, but this is not Christmas."

Townsen began pacing back and forth.

"I ought to bust your ass for obstruction of justice and whatever else I can find. That's what I ought to do." Townsen said in frustration.

Harris laughed. "You'll never make any of these lame trumped-up charges stick, especially on me."

"Well, how about taking money from the Mafia for feeding them tons of classified information? I can sure as hell make that charge stick even on a squeaky-clean cop."

Harris knew the only person who could make such an accusation was Mr. C and he had been dead for months. Harris responded as he shook his head. "You're pulling this out of your hat, right? Is that how you do it? You have nothing of the sort and we both know it."

He laughed, hoping that there was no such evidence.

"You start talking or we'll find out in five seconds or so. The paperwork is lying on my desk just in case there's some foul play that delays my return"

Reynolds drew his 9-millimeter semi-automatic pistol. He chambered a round and shuddered realizing that if matters got any worse, Harris' plan would force him to kill a federal agent. He extended his arm and aimed through the concealing foliage at Townsen's head.

"Otis, this is all crazy. You know I'm not that kind of guy. I don't have any idea about your boy. Why would you think such a thing about me?"

Harris sported a big grin as if they had been long-time buddies. He stepped closer with an open handed display of feigned confusion.

"Call it a hunch." Townsen had been an FBI agent for over twenty years and he had learned that the behavior of most would not conceal their lies.

Earlier he had caught Harris' comment about *someone taking out a big-time local Mafia crook*. No one had ever mentioned anything like that nor was there anything about it circulating on the street. In fact the streets were too quite. Something was definitely going on and Harris knew something. Hell, Townsen though, Harris probably did the deed, else why that particular comment?

Now he was finally convinced that Detective Harris was indeed dirty.

"Well, I'd dump that source if I were you. It's not reliable. That's the end of this private discussion."

Harris turned and began walking to his car.

Townsen raised his voice. "Harris, when I can prove you're involved in any of this I will file charges and I will nail your ass, Mister."

📖

Early fall at *The Desert Phoenix* was more like the middle of summer. It was 3:40 p.m.

The temperature still hovered around one hundred and the humidity was nearly as high. An ocean breeze provided them some comfort, but gallons of ice tea provided much more.

Most clustered on the veranda. Small groups lounged. In the heat they sought what little shade they could find and reminisced about their past interaction with papa.

Occasional tears arrived.

Jerry and Doug sat in the shade near the south end of the veranda. A servant had just brought their third bottle of beer to them. Jerry's tears had flowed earlier, but now were temporarily under control.

"Doug, I really envy you. Papa saw so much potential in you that he went out of his way more than once to accommodate your feelings not to be involved in any of our family's questionable or illegal activities."

Through a look of surprise Doug responded.

"I didn't know that. He made me believe that I had to fight for each and every concession I sought."

"That's how he wanted it, nothing was ever to be given to anyone for free, not to me nor you. More than once he expressed praise for you regarding the personal confidence and ethics you demonstrated so easily."

Doug nodded feeling a bit choked up then he added.

"Your papa was quite an unusual man."

For a moment Jerry could not find his voice. "He was."

Sammy approached the men and sat in a towel-draped

decorative wrought iron chair next to Doug.

As their hands intertwined neither spoke.

Then Kely approached to take a seat next to Jerry. "How you feeling, honey?"

Her lips brushed his ear.

Finally he managed to offer a smile. "I'm okay, but this will not be remembered as one of my best days."

To avoid having Townsen see them leave together, Harris and Reynolds waited another ten minutes before getting on the road.

The drive back to West LA was long.

Neither man spoke much.

The long delays of commute traffic added to their boredom. Occasionally Harris swore at other drivers and threatened two of them with going to court if he ever saw them again.

Finally Reynolds built up courage to question him.

"Do you really think we can pull this off?"

"Sure. What makes you ask that?"

"That federal agent didn't seem to like you very much. He looks like real trouble to me." Reynolds confided.

"Don't worry about him. He's harmless. He's been on my case like that for a couple of years."

Townsen was still on the road, too.

Contemplating what Harris' next move might be, he

dialed Agent Wilson's number on his car phone.

In a moment he answered. "Hello."

"This is Townsen. I need you to walk softly with this request, but find out what Detective Harris is working on. I'll need chapter and verse and I need it yesterday."

"Yes, sir. I'll call you back later tonight with it."

"By the way, use the authority of BD-909 and pull his banking records for the last ten years. Cross-reference the results with IRS files and tabulate them in your report by years. Carlson says he's been on the take for much longer, so I'd expect to see a big gap in the numbers." He paused.

"Sir, are you sure that you want to create that kind of a paper trail? 909 requires us to file too many docs with the Justice Department. It won't be forty-eight hours until the Chief of Police has them, too."

Townsen cringed at the thought. "I know and I'm kind of hoping that these hints at a scandal will force someone's hand. I want him out of my hair and hopefully this will be enough to do it."

Wilson was not convinced. "That police board is too weak to make such a high profile move, sir. We might be riling too many feathers with such a move until we have the evidence in our hands. I'd be a little more cautious with this sort of thing, if I were you, sir."

There was silence.

Agent Townsen laid the phone on the seat as he contemplated the situation and continued driving. Several times Wilson tried to get his attention.

After a minute he picked up the phone and spoke.

"You're right, Wilson. Go ahead and pull the data through covert channels and block any retention of the inquiry. Under the circumstances we'll have to treat him as if he's an active member of the Mafia."

Chapter Twelve

Jerry spoke. "I can't believe he would attempt something as personally dangerous and stupid as this."

"Well, believe it. I'm certain it was him. I looked him straight in his eyes while this was all happening."

Sammy and Kely sat at the same table, but carried on a much different conversation than the guys.

"Okay. How would you take care of this?" Jerry asked of Doug without expecting a serious answer.

"Easy, we report it to the police and let them handle it. That's their job, remember?"

Jerry laughed.

"Did all of your common sense drain out when they bashed your head, buddy? That kind of report about papa would never fly with the LAPD."

Doug thought about it for a moment before responding. "So are you saying that the police won't take us serious because Bruno was the intended target?"

"That's it. For us to any get serious justice against Harris he would have had to kill mama and half of the family at the very same time."

Doug nodded as he took a sip of cold beer.

Jerry continued.

"And even then I'd be hesitant to really believe that he'd ever pay properly for what he's done."

"Isn't that a bit of a jaded view about the police?" Doug asked. "You must know there are many honest men and women working on the force."

"The practice of honesty is only a part of what justice is about." Jerry knew that lies could convict as easily as the truth, if repeated often enough by the right people.

Doug felt it necessary to repeat himself.

"I still say it's a bit paranoid."

"Probably, but I don't think it's much different than what you felt last year with Mr. C, is it?"

"That's a good point, but also a bit different."

"I don't think so. You were minutes away from having a professional hit put on you that no one could have undone." Doug nodded and Jerry continued.

"Here we have a rogue cop who's turned on us and practicing what he knows best. We can't just waltz down to the nearest police station and report him as you suggest. He'll deny it and then probably make counter charges against us that'll most likely stick."

Doug shook his head. "I was afraid of something like this, another of my famous no-win situations."

"Sorry, pal, but that's the hand we've got to play."

Doug was befuddled.

"Okay, how does all of this look to you?"

Jerry was quick with his answer.

"We either set him up in some kind of a sting operation or we just take him out. One is quick and dirty. The other will take us some time."

"Wait a minute. You're talking about killing a cop. Is that the only kind of solution you can think about?"

"Sometimes legal solutions aren't worth talking about because nothing gets done for years."

Doug retorted. "I'm uncomfortable even talking like this when the subject is killing a cop."

"That's how this particular problem has been defined by Harris. Don't forget, this is the same cop who tried to kill us and did succeed in killing several others not to mention my papa."

Doug could not argue with the words. They echoed endlessly in his head. Instead of responding, he took his half-full bottle of beer and chugged it.

Sammy glimpsed his behavior and slid her chair closer. "What's wrong, Doug, that didn't look good to me."

He turned away, took a deep breath and just sat there shaking his head.

She spoke sternly to Jerry. "What's happening here?"

"We were talking about how to handle the situation with Harris and his men."

With growing concern Kely asked. "That's the cop who is behind all of this, right?"

Jerry nodded.

Julia approached them. "It's time for dinner, guys."

Doug turned back toward Sammy and said. "Jerry and I have to go back to LA for Harris."

Horror rushed over Kely's face. "No, not again, not now. You don't have to do that, do you, Doug?"

He turned to her. "I've got to do it and I want the two of you to understand the reasons why."

Kely replied. "No Doug, not this time. Just let it go. You can do that, can't you?"

Her hand reached for him.

Several tears rolled down his face. Sammy reached for his other hand. Julia sat in an adjacent chair. Kely was ready to demand that he give it up when he responded.

"Kely, I can't let it go. Not now. I just found out that Harris is the person responsible for giving Katy's address to Mr. C's people last year."

She gasped and tears immediately welled in her eyes.

Sammy shifted her attention to Kely.

Kely's determination not to give in had reddened her face. "I don't care, Doug. That's in the past. As much as it hurts me to hear about it at a time like this, I want you to stay alive for me, for all of us and for Sammy."

Sammy asked. "What exactly does this mean?"

He looked toward Jerry who held up his hands, so Doug responded. "Well, for now we're not exactly sure. We'll be getting some payback from Harris and the other guys who helped him with all of this."

Finally Julia spoke. "Doug, this isn't something you or Jerry need to do. There are others who'll do a difficult job like this, maybe for free, just because it was papa."

She looked toward Jerry and he nodded.

"And I'm one of them." Doug responded sharply. His mind was numbed by such thoughts.

For months he had hesitated to allow his feelings about

Bruno to be expressed. Never quite accepting that Bruno, the friendly, loving family man, was also Bruno, *The Godfather* of the Los Angeles Mafia. The paradox still gripped him, but he knew this was something he had to do just like last December.

Jerry nodded, then spoke through tight lips. "Me, too."

📖

Agent Wilson walked into Townsen's office and spoke to him. "Sir, I've got some bad news for you."

Townsen stopped working and looked up. "Okay."

"It seems Harris has had no field assignments for the past few months. For now he's an office supervisor."

"Interesting. Any problem getting the info?"

Agent Wilson offered a faint smile. "Nope. I just identified myself and asked. It was all boringly routine."

"What about his bank account?" Townsen asked.

"It looks exactly like what you expected, sir. Every month since 1981, there was a cash deposit of at least a thousand dollars. It has been as high as twenty-five hundred, but it all stopped in January of this year. Not a single extra dime has been deposited since then."

Townsen looked puzzled. "Any reasons for that?"

"No, sir, but his savings is currently suffering a similar hit each month. He's depleted it by $13, 175 just since the first of the year."

Townsen leaned back in his chair and sighed. "Interesting. If like Carlson says, he was on the mob's payroll, it looks as if he isn't on it now."

Wilson nodded.

📖

Bruno's company jet landed in San Diego at 12:20 p.m. sharp. Earlier in the flight orders had been given to Carlos, the butler. The bodyguards, the chauffeurs and two domestic servants also accompanied them. When the plane landed Carlos took charge of the rest of the party.

A commercial flight had just arrived and the mass of travelers masked their arrival.

Escorted by four of their bodyguards, Jerry and Doug went directly to a private lounge in the airport that they had reserved for a meeting to be held at two o'clock. After they checked out the room, it was setup to accommodate all of the Mafia family heads from Los Angeles.

By 1:50 they had all been seated.

Both men remained out of sight during the arrival of the patriarchs. Rumors that Bruno had been injured or killed in an auto accident were rampant and they did not want to face such questions until they could answer them with the proper amount of respect, dignity and detail.

While Doug waited in a nearby lounge, Jerry walked into the room to begin the meeting. Flanked by bodyguards he walked to the head of the table and without hesitation took Bruno's usual position. Looks of surprise and murmurs shot back and forth among the men around the table. Several of the patriarch's bodyguards standing along the wall straightened and focused their full attention on Jerry.

He raised his hands and spoke to the group.

"Excuse me, gentlemen. May I have your attention? There are important matters we must handle today."

There was silence.

Jerry peered long into the faces of the men who had held his father's trust for so many years. Now he needed to rely on them and the enduring strength of that trust.

"Forgive me, because this afternoon I bring you very sad news." All eyes focused more intently on him.

He paused, fighting to maintain his composure. Finally, he was able to speak. "This past Monday evening there was an assassination attempt on papa."

The room erupted with groans and exclamations of disbelief. Again Jerry raised his hands to muster the silence he sought before he could continue.

"At 1:03 yesterday morning my papa, Bruno Alfonso Sebastino, died from injuries he received during that unprovoked and vicious attack."

Again the room erupted, but now with anger, disbelief and expressions of condolence.

Several rose from the table as if leaving.

Bodyguards moved closer to their charges. To many it looked as if the meeting was over.

Jerry reacted to the confusion.

"Gentlemen, keep your seats so I can continue. Please allow me the respect of finishing my statement."

After several seconds all returned to their seats.

He continued. "Before papa died he made provisions for the company to continue its operations without interruption. The exact language is contained in documents filed with Jay Feldman. Today I am here to plead with you in papa's name for a peaceful transition.

"Gentlemen, my father asks that you accept and appoint the esteemed honorable Joseph Richard Baldevino to fill his now vacant company position."

Most at the table displayed their surprise.

Mr. Baldevino looked around the table as if to suggest he was equally stunned. At age 61 he was experienced, well liked and dependable. While not Bruno's first choice, under the circumstances he was the best person for the job and one of the few men who could unify the family in these times of pending crisis.

"As an incentive Jay will transfer from papa's personal funds the sum of five million dollars to each and every family head who supports his wishes and continues to faithfully do so for at least the next six months."

Gasps were heard around the table.

Again Jerry raised his hand for silence.

It did not work.

Quick mental calculations by several of the men at the table made them realize that such amounts yielded a pay-out of over 100 million dollars. It was very nice for them, but few knew how wealthy Bruno had become during the past few months.

He raised his voice. "Please, my dear friends. There are other items of importance to be discussed."

Several small groups conferred among themselves.

Silence came slowly.

"If papa's request is acceptable, please so signify."

A number of the men leaned to his neighbor and conferred about the practicality of both making and then accepting such an unusual offer. Someone whispered that even in death Bruno's generosity continued to bless them. As each man arrived at a decision he turned and offered an appropriate hand signal of approval to Jerry.

"Additionally papa asked that the following allowances

be made for the continued support of his family.

"First, that all of the family real estate and personal funds currently held in his name shall be transferred in total for the benefit of his surviving family members. Next, that all company assets under his control at the time of his death shall be turned over to Mr. Baldevino for distribution to the heads of all of the other families of Los Angeles in whatever manner he believes to be fair and equitable."

A new buzz filled the air.

Such a disposition had seldom occurred in the past. It was usual for a son to continue in the business of his father. All knew that Jerry's statements meant he was giving up that right in order to provide a benefit to them.

"If acceptable, please so signify."

Each member nodded.

"Gentlemen, for the next few days I will coordinate an operation from safe house #423. It is designed to bring the man responsible for papa's death to instant justice. The man's name is Detective Jason Harris of the Los Angeles Police Department. Please forward all information that's gathered about this person and his whereabouts to me on a 24-hour basis. Are there any questions?"

"Please, excuse me, Jerry." Mr. Baldevino begged. "I was approached by Detective Harris a few months ago. He suggested that I add a new line of business with what he called our leap into the lucrative *hi-tech piracy* market. For my involvement I told him no. Do you know if that proposal was ever presented to Bruno and did he ever make a determination about it?"

"Yes. It was and papa refused to allow such expansions of the business. Didn't Mr. Marcello ever disperse the details of that meeting to the rest of you?"

All heads turned to focus on Cecil Marcello. Their eyes lingered on his youthful good looks.

He did not respond.

Mr. Baldevino asked him directly. "Marty, did you ever discuss the details of this venture with Bruno?"

Cecil shrugged his shoulders and spoke without thinking. "Yeah, maybe. Well, actually I don't remember if we ever did or not. That was about the time Julio was graduated from USC. My mind was distracted by a lot of other things during that period of time."

There were a number of looks of confusion around the table. Two of the men shook their heads in disbelief.

Cecil had been a family head for less than a year. The death of his father was mourned by many, but Cecil's elevation to such a lofty position with all of the associated status was praised by few and disliked by many. Although raised in a wealthy family, the pursuit of even more wealth had become his biggest motivation.

Mr. Baldevino turned to Jerry. "Do you happen to remember when all of this occurred?"

"Let's see, today's the 28th. It must have been eight to ten weeks ago during some of the hottest days of the summer." Jerry referred to a calendar in his coat jacket. "I'd say it was in the first half of July." He nodded. "Something like that for sure, but not any earlier."

Again the group turned to look at Cecil.

He just sat, smiled sheepishly and did not respond.

Someone whispered loud enough for all to hear. "I smell a rat." Several nodded at the implication.

"Marty, this isn't looking too good for you. Do you

have anything to say for yourself?" Mr. Baldevino asked.

Cecil looked around the room before finally speaking. "I swear I had nothing whatsoever to do with any plans for a hit like this on Bruno."

He fidgeted in his chair when Mr. Baldevino waved one of his own bodyguards toward Cecil's bodyguard. All watched as the young man gave up a concealed pistol.

"Why do you call it a hit, Marty?" Jerry asked.

He shrugged his shoulders again and started to stutter. "Well, I uh… just thought that uh… well, you know. That's how we had talked about it earlier uh… today."

Mr. Baldevino's bodyguards moved behind Cecil. He turned to look at them as he began to speak. "Come on, now, Joe. Let's don't get carried away. There must be a reasonable explanation for all of this."

With open hands Mr. Baldevino asked. "Okay, let's hear about it, Marty, if you think one exists."

Those sitting close to him saw him begin to sweat.

He arranged some papers on the table in front of him then leaned back in his chair before he responded.

"Yeah, I had contact with Jason, but only like most of the rest of you did. That does not mean we were scheming against Bruno or anything like that, does it?"

He searched for a handkerchief to wipe his face.

"Not exactly, but you are the only one to take the issue to Bruno. The rest of us told him no from the very start so why didn't you do the same?"

Many nodded as they stared at Cecil.

He hunted for words before he spoke. "It seemed like a very good idea to me at the time. Everyone knows that our piece of the local pie is getting smaller every day. What with the Blacks, the Asians, and now the Russians, there's no room for us to grow or expand into new areas. Building a new source of income was my only reason for doing it. When Bruno said no, I dropped the whole idea. That's the *honest to god* truth, just ask anybody." He motioned around the room with his hand.

No one volunteered a response in his defense.

"Come on, guys. That's the way it was, right?"

Again no one responded.

Mr. Baldevino asked. "What exactly did you tell this Detective Harris about Bruno's unwillingness to proceed with his grandiose plans?"

Anxiously Cecil responded. "I told him exactly what had happened. That Bruno had nixed the idea. That's all." He raised his hand as if to swear to his statement.

"And what was Detective Harris' response?"

"He was pissed that I wouldn't take the responsibility to do it on my own. But I told him in no uncertain terms that Bruno didn't run the company like that. We all did exactly as Bruno dictated. And that as long as Bruno was the head of the LA Branch it wouldn't ever happen. That was it. I never encouraged him to do anything else."

Mr. Baldevino waved his hand and the bodyguards lifted Cecil from his chair.

He complained. "Mr. Baldevino, come on. This isn't right. Please. You know it isn't. There was nothing I could do at the time. I had no idea he would consider doing something as foolish as this."

Mr. Baldevino nodded and motioned for both Cecil and his bodyguard to be led from the room.

Neither protested further.

Turning his attention to the other men seated at the table he asked. "How much of what we heard is true?"

Alfred, a thin balding man with big wire rim glasses, responded. "I don't believe much of what I just heard from Cecil. There have been rumors of this new venture of his on the street as recent as just last week."

Several others nodded.

Mr. Baldevino sighed. "I was afraid that something like this would happen. I'd heard them, too, but thought Bruno had given the orders to start setting it up."

He shook his head and asked Jerry. "Before we can proceed with any more business, there is another matter that must be settled first."

Looking at Bruno's ring on his finger, Jerry stood as a bodyguard moved his seat to a corner of the room.

"Considering the circumstances, gentlemen, we will have to improvise the ceremony. Before we get started send someone out to buy the finest available brandy."

Alfred's bodyguards were dispatched with the task.

Jerry took the honored seat for Bruno.

Each patriarch in turn passed in front of him and kissed the cherished ring. It was a display of respect for Bruno. To Jerry, it was his final act in the company business.

Mr. Baldevino was the last one in the line. He bowed to kiss the ring and as he stood so did Jerry.

Standing face to face, with the empty chair to their side, a moment of silence filled the room. The other patriarchs stood shoulder to shoulder and formed a semicircle on the other side of the two men.

The bodyguards remained in the back of the room.

Pausing to feel the moment, Jerry removed the ring and

stepped forward placing a kiss on each of Mr. Baldevino's cheeks. After stepping back he placed the ring in the palm of the hand of the new Don.

"This ring is a symbol of our love, trust and devotion to you, as the ultimate authority in our family. It makes you accountable only to the almighty God. We offer our undying support to you and pledge that your words shall become our law."

Mr. Baldevino slipped the ring onto the second finger of his right hand. Slowly he took his place in the empty chair and starting with Jerry each of the patriarchs again passed in front of him and kissed the ring.

When the ceremony was concluded, each man took a seat at the table. Jerry offered the head chair to Mr. Baldevino, but he declined saying. "For today I would be honored if you would accept that seat in my place as a tribute to my dear friend, Bruno."

From a seat on the side of the table Mr. Baldevino asked for a decision. "Gentlemen, how shall we handle the matter of Cecil Marcello, his associates and their actions with Detective Harris?"

Slowly Mr. Baldevino's eyes focused on each man sitting around the table. When each man gave his signal he moved to the next one. This part of the decision making process would never be spoken.

After several minutes he nodded, then spoke to Jerry.

"Mr. Sebastino, you may continue."

"That was all I had to say, thank-you. Gentlemen, I wish each of you a long life, good health and a happy home and family." Jerry stood.

Each man at the table did the same.

One by one Bruno's lifetime friends passed in front of Jerry to offer their condolences. They had many questions of concern for mama and the rest of the family, warm handshakes, hugs and even a few brief tears.

Twenty minutes later the farewell toast to Bruno was made by all the remaining Mafia patriarchs of LA. Five minutes later a toast was made to the new Don.

At 3:35 four limousines drove north toward Los Angeles and the safe house. Now Doug and Jerry could begin the serious task of planning how they would dispense their brand of instant justice to Harris.

Chapter Thirteen

An administrator, a cook and an armed guard permanently staffed the grounds of safe house #423. Within an hour of Jerry's announcement about Detective Harris, fifteen men were assigned by Mr. Baldevino to track his every action. His code name was *Badboy*.

Twelve minutes later the first report arrived. It read:

Badboy located and is heading west at 55 miles per hour on the Santa Monica Freeway.

📖

"LA Crime Unit, Townsen speaking."

"Sir, this is Wilson. I just spotted Shorty Johnson tailing Detective Harris. Doesn't he sometimes work for one of the men in Bruno Sebastino's organization?"

"I think you're right, Wilson. What's happening?"

"I picked up Harris at the precinct. After tailing him for ten minutes I finally made Shorty's vehicle. He's tailing Harris, too and doing it like a real pro."

Townsen pushed his chair back and leaned into the wall. A deep breath faded into a smile. "Well, it seems to be looking a lot like Christmas after all."

"Sir?" Wilson's voice lingered.

With an unusual sense of delight in his voice Townsen issued orders. "Wilson, take off early this afternoon. I'll see you in the office tomorrow morning."

📖

The limousines were exchanged for white vans with darkened windows several miles from the safe house. At 6:05 p.m. the vehicle with Doug and Jerry pulled into the garage of #423. The others would drop off their passengers at various times over the next few hours so the neighbors would not become suspicious.

They planned for only one van to be present at the house at any one particular time.

Doug and Jerry went straight to their rooms overlooking the quiet street. The two-story house sat near the end of the block and projected the image of respectable middle class suburban owners. A smaller cottage behind the garage housed the permanent staff. Two lockable cells had been dug and constructed under the main house.

Storage lockers in the garage held the weapons. Only the security guard and personal bodyguards could have weapons in the house.

Within a half-hour they sat at the dining room table getting acquainted with the resources of the facility. Two different phone lines were installed in the house. One would be dedicated to tracking Harris' location on a personal computer. It would also be used to log, analyze and print reports detailing his doings and whereabouts. The printed log was already three pages in length.

The task of compiling a dossier on Harris had been started several hours earlier by Curt Fraiser, a recent UCLA graduate who was also very well versed in handling the new computer. He handed the report to Jerry.

"I don't get it." Curt wondered aloud. "Inside the PD this guy is practically a poster boy. Why would he toss all of that for a shot at taking out Bruno?"

"Money. He wanted money out of us, a lot of it." Jerry said as he opened the folder and began reading the summary Curt had written.

Jason Robert Harris. Twenty-one years on the LAPD. Married Pamela Louise Tester in 1968. Three grown children. Hired by Mr. deCasale in 1974 at $2,500/mon. Payments ceased Dec. of 89 upon death of Mr. deCasale.

"Is he really that clean?" Doug inquired.

Jerry scanned several more pages before he answered. "He seems to be. The brass at the PD probably don't have a clue about our cash payments to this loose-lipped cop."

Doug nodded. "What about his partners?"

Curt looked confused but responded. "Currently I don't have any names for the others. Who are they? I'll have their data for you by morning."

Jerry thought for a moment.

"I can see their faces as plain as day, but I'm drawing a blank on their names."

He looked quizzically toward Doug.

Doug was certain about his response. "I've never seen either of them before."

He paused a moment and continued. "But I'm sure I'd recognize them if I ever saw them again."

Jerry added with confidence. "I'm sure they're both stationed with him at the same precinct."

Before he finished talking Curt was already typing on the keyboard. "I'll have those by morning."

Doug inquired. "Have we decided how to do it yet?"

"Not me, pal. You got any ideas?" Jerry smiled.

"Well, I agree with earlier comments and those two options. We either make him look dirty or we make it look like an accident. If he's in prison he'll be despised and he might get into more trouble. If it's an accident it's over for good and we bury the guy and these memories. That's the end of the problem and the one I'd select."

"I also like the second one best. It's done and we can forget about his miserable antics."

Playfully Jerry winked at Curt who had been following their discussion from the corner of his eye. Curt hastily turned his face to hide the red glow he sported and resumed his activity on the computer.

"Or we can make it look like one of his partners did it. Harris is still buried and his partner goes to the joint for it." Doug added.

"That still leaves us with another partner to handle. Papa never liked loose ends." Jerry commented.

"Okay, it looks like accidents all around. Can you live with that?" Doug asked.

"As long as I can be involved in making them happen."

Doug leaned forward. "Good. How does this all sound? First, I'd like to get...."

Chapter Fourteen

The out of the way location of *The Sandman Restaurant and Pub* made it ideal for their private dinner. Doug and Jerry had parked at 8:32 p.m. Their bodyguards took their meal sitting at a nearby table. Curt was ordered to call them immediately, if Harris or any of his men approached the area and especially the restaurant. Jerry had voiced a willingness to finally relax a bit, but Doug cautioned him against it.

As their meals arrived Doug finished his drink and ordered another for each of them. He decided to change the subject to something more personal.

"Jerry, you and Kely certainly do make a very lovely couple. I think she's absolutely beamed since you presented her with that diamond ring."

He smiled as he reached for his bottle.

"I think you're right. Even with all this upset, she handles it so wonderfully. Sammy seems to be a damn-good support person for her."

"Be careful, they call it sisterhood, remember?" Both men laughed. Doug proceeded. "They do get along so much like sisters, don't they?"

"That's for sure."

Doug continued eating, but silence loomed nearby and soon gripped him without warning. His mind brought-forth wonderful images of being with Catherine. Every brief glance of Kely's similar beauty reminded his still wounded heart of those happy days. He would never speak of it to her, but the pain still came.

Now with the recent death of Bruno his pain and doubts stirred deeper feelings. He felt like ripping out his aching heart for just one day of uninterrupted peace.

Sensing his mood, Jerry asked. "What's wrong? I think I've seen those menacing clouds around you before."

Doug nodded, then started explaining the reason for his distraction. "I've tried several times in the past few weeks to ask Sammy to marry me, but every time I get close to actually doing it, memories from the past bombard me with all that painful stuff. Then before I know it I'm out of the mood and I lose my nerve."

"Sounds like a tough place to be, buddy." Jerry pursed his lips and shook his head in sympathy.

Doug nodded.

"I get paranoid that she'll want to be involved in something that'll get her killed like Catherine. This situation with Harris has me really bummed, even though it's considerably different than with Mr. C."

Jerry asked. "How's that? It all looks the same to me."

He smiled, as he reached to take another drink of beer.

"When dealing with Mr. C I felt as if the entire Mafia would soon be united and then come after me as a group."

Jerry smiled at Doug's image of the underworld.

Doug continued. "To me that meant that the situation would never end until they either had me dead and buried or I managed to flee the country. Now, the worst case seems to be surviving the confrontation and possibly going to prison, if I get caught for killing Harris and his cop buddies. After what they've done, this is quite a bit different than fighting with the mob and being dumped in an unmarked grave. At least I'll still be alive this time if I can get past the battles with him and his cronies."

Jerry smiled at Doug's detailed analysis. "It certainly seems like you're better off now when you look at it that way." Jerry shook his head. "But that wouldn't have ever occurred to me."

"That's part of the reason I'm so pleased the girls decided to stay in Cabo a while longer." Doug confided.

"Me, too. I feel better not having them exposed to any of this, especially if we're moving out of the family business. In a perfect world we wouldn't have to be dealing with any of this at all."

Doug remembered being in college and all the nonsense talk about living in a perfect world. He smiled slyly. "Yep, that would be nice, but this behavior certainly raises tough questions. I'll be pleased if we can just keep our own lives in better shape."

Jerry nodded. "Our own connections and the closeness of the girls are good signs. Don't you think?" Doug nodded. "Did I ever mention that Kely once said, the main reason she's drawn so strongly to Sammy is because she has that same fire and pursuit of life as Catherine? Once she even commented to me that you probably couldn't love another woman who had any less, even if you tried."

Nodding again, Doug's mind found a hidden image of Catherine. Her wide beautiful smile called out to his heart. Wonderful recollections from their last few days flooded him. His inner voice shouted Sammy's name, but the rest of his willing thoughts consciously conspired to withhold her face. The battle raged.

It was now mind against heart and no prisoners would be taken in that emotional war.

"Snap out of it, Doug." Jerry leaned forward and in a brotherly way touched his friends forearm. "This stuff is really getting a strange hold on you, isn't it?"

Doug nodded and reached for his fork. He was not ready to discuss it just yet. He took a bite of his entrée.

"I had no idea." Jerry's concern shifted to pride. He recalled watching Doug's valiant display of grit and determination on that Vietnam battlefield where he completely disregarded his own safety in order to secure it for others.

Now, Doug displayed that same level of devotion for a lost love, one he was helpless to save at the time and was now fearful for a new love he might not be able to protect. He smiled, savoring the wonderfully painful dilemmas of the heart in the uncharted matters of love.

He smiled at Doug's heroism and their close friendship, but continued eating. After a couple of minutes of silence he spoke again to Doug. "You feeling any better?"

"A bit."

The sound of Doug's voice reinforced the tone of his

noncommittal words. Jerry added. "You know, buddy, I'm surprised at you. For being a genuine, hard as rocks, battle-tested jarhead you're really a softy at some things. Can you explain that bit of paradox?"

Doug shook his head while taking a long drink of water. "Sometimes I just can't keep thoughts of Catherine out of my head. Sounds pretty weird, huh?"

"Not really. It just sounds to me like your heart is not fully healed from that intense level of devotion. It probably requires you getting on with the rest of your life to make it feel a little easier."

"I know." Doug sighed. Their eyes met in a stare.

His seriousness was reinforced in his words. "But first I have to get back my warrior mentality. To do that I'll have to give up everything for a few days, maybe longer."

Jerry's eyes widened since he was not completely sure of what he had just heard. "Well, I think you're right; that's exactly what we have to do."

"You're wrong, friend. I have to do this alone. Some of this face to face activity is not for you. You do your stuff in the command center and I'll do the grunt work in the field. How does that sound?"

Hesitating a moment Jerry nodded. "That's pretty much how I was thinking about it, too."

Doug looked at his watch, felt like yawning, but fought the urge. "Good. Let's move to the bar for a little while."

📖

By 10:30 the patronage at *The Watering Hole* had dwindled considerably, but Harris and Reynolds still remained. They both had drank too many tequila poppers and it had begun to show.

Now, playing and betting with the dice consumed their thoughts. With over forty dollars of cash on the table in front of them, the rumbling of the dice and the sound of the dice cup slamming hard against the table echoed throughout the small tavern.

As usual Reynolds was losing. "You're one lucky son-of-a-bitch." He yelled at Harris.

"If you weren't so damn drunk, you'd be playing a whole lot better." Harris retorted and grabbed a quick sip of his *JD on the rocks*.

A beer chaser sat nearby, if needed. It was not.

In the distance the barmaid prepared another round of poppers. Reynolds tossed the dice into the cup, blew hard into the cup and started to shake them.

"Come on, baby. Line up those sixes." After one last shake he slammed the cup to the table.

Pausing he tilted the cup slightly to peek at his numbers. He saw a six and yanked it to expose the others, two sixes, a five and two fours.

He shouted. "All right! Finally lady luck is here." Then he tossed two more dollars in the center of the table.

Harris matched the bet, retrieved the dice and prepared to play. The barmaid arrived and began setting the new round of drinks in front of each man.

He tossed a ten-dollar bill onto her tray. She prepared to count out his change, but Harris waved her away with an almost obscene male grunt of approval.

Both men placed their hand over the tequila-filled shot glass topped with a cocktail napkin, grasped it, raised it about a foot and then slammed it to the table.

The two impacts sounded like one.

Immediately they downed the shot and reached for a mug of beer. Reynolds chugged the full ten ounces.

Harris finished half of his, then picked up the dice cup, shook it and slammed it hard onto the table.

📖

The van pulled into the driveway of #423.

Its darkened windows reflected the glare from the headlights. Entering the back door they headed for the stairs. An unusual glow came from the dining room.

They diverted to inspect it.

Curt was asleep in front of his computer.

The gentle radiance of the screen bathed the room in grays just short of noticeable shadows. Looking close at the *Badboy* log, it seemed that Curt had stopped typing in the middle of a sentence.

Jerry pointed it out to Doug and both men chuckled.

The last six entries indicated that Harris was currently drinking with a friend at a broken-down nightclub located near his precinct.

"What do you think? Shall we check this out or get a good nights sleep?"

Doug chuckled slyly and responded. "I'm game if you are." He wrote the address on a yellow sticky and grabbed a city map to find it.

Jerry roused Curt and he jerked into awareness.

They reviewed the log. Clearly the situation was well under control. Four men still worked on the stakeout. Two members of the tail were actually inside of the bar observing Harris directly from across the room.

They had not had nearly as much to drink.

In the garage Doug found a sniper rifle with ten rounds of ammo and a 9-millimeter pistol with two full clips of hollow-point shells.

He placed them both in the van, tuned the portable citizen band radio to channel 38 and picked up the mike.

"*Charlie-one*, this is *night-light*. Do you copy?"

There was silence.

Momentarily the portable radio snapped to life.

"Doug, is that you?"

There were several extra clicks as if Jerry was trying to get the hang of it by pressing them all.

"Great, so much for your radio procedure."

"Oh… this is *Charlie-one*. We copy you… four by four, uh… that's loud and clear… *night-light*."

"*Charlie-one*, much better. Proceeding to location."

📖

The early morning temperature held in the mid-fifties. Surface street traffic was almost nonexistent. Although it was late Doug did not feel tired.

Finally his thoughts of being alone were fulfilled. With so much to sort through, he preferred it that way.

He turned onto the street where *The Watering Hole* was located. It was 1:32 a.m.

Doug was pleased that there had been no other air-traffic on channel 38 during the whole drive. He reached for the CB's microphone.

"*Charlie-one*, the *night-light* is on."

Shortly the response came.

"*Badboy* status unchanged."

"Thanks, good buddy. Proceeding as planned." He hung the mike on the receiver and lowered the volume.

He stopped the van directly across the street in front of the shabby tavern. It was situated between two larger buildings with a narrow lane on each side for parking access to the back of the building.

Dim streetlights shined in the distance. Dancing shadows draped the entrance. *Not a place to take a date.*

Three cars were parked on the street at the front door.

Doug pulled into one of the driveways and drove to the rear parking area. It was actually darker there than in front of the building. Six vehicles lined a rear wall. He wondered which one belonged to Harris.

He picked up the CB.

"*Charlie-one*, request data on *Badboy's* ride?"

After a very long pause he got his report. "Two x-ray pee eye duck. Roger."

Doug smiled at the cryptic response then chuckled, but now he had to decipher it.

Through a happy smile he began sorting the possible messages. *Two x-ray... 2 X... 2 times... 2 years... 2 years old. Pee eye... polished immaculate... plainly inhibited... oh, that's it... police issue. That makes sense. Duck... truck... there were no trucks... duck... duck... Dodge. That's it... a two years old, police issue Dodge.*

He grinned broadly at the results.

A quick scan of nearby cars indicated it was not parked in the back. He drove to the street and prepared to park near the westerly corner. There was the Dodge parked on the street by the driveway with a Kojak light sitting in the middle of the dash.

He grabbed the mike and clicked it to transmit.

"PI duck spotted. Real cute, *Charlie-one*."

Doug sighed, leaned back and stretched out his legs.

Now the waiting would begin.

With little effort his thoughts found Sammy's beautiful face and the uniqueness of that last sunset they had shared on the veranda in Cabo.

After most others had retired to the house, they remained near the chiseled stone railing overlooking the cliff and the Pacific Ocean.

The roar of the breakers far below on the rocks framed the boundaries of his memory. The touch of the stone rail still held some of the day's heat.

Breezes brushed their sandaled toes.

Cherubs smiled at them from a distance. Standing hand in hand their anticipating fingers intermingled. Shared warmth shielded a furtive night breeze.

Clouds in the northwest proclaimed the heavy midnight rain to come in a few hours. Due west its fringes danced and frolicked with the setting rays of sunlight. Deep reds, oranges and yellows painted the sky. Such extremes broadcast a breath-stopping natural beauty.

Doug had appreciated sensations like this many times and of course Sammy had also seen them before, but now she stopped to be a part of it all.

The conversation was mostly whispers of praise for the final good-bye of the day that God had so lovingly painted in the sky. Doug's mind sought the proper words for his heart to make a moonlight proposal, but they failed to materialize in his throat.

He jumped in surprise when Jerry's voice brought the CB to life. "*Night-light*, status check."

Looking at his watch, it was one minute until two, then he responded. "Charlie-one, no change."

"By the way, the entire location is now confirmed to be pee eye." Jerry's voice boomed.

"Affirmative, *Charlie-one*. See you in twenty."

Doug started the van and drove slowly forward.

The doors of the tavern swung open.

Light bathed the badly aged, weathered and cracked sidewalk. A stream of stupored men exited, lingered for a moment and formed into several after-hours groups.

None looked toward him.

He drove past them without looking at them either.

Chapter Fifteen

Doug's bedside phone rang.

He jerked from the sudden sound, reached for it and managed to mumble through his broken slumber.

"Hello."

Sammy's cheerful voice pulled him to full awareness. "What's this, Mister? It's 10:30 in the morning and you're not awake yet?" She enjoyed finding him asleep for once.

He fabricated an excuse.

"Jerry kept me out too late last night. You know how much he likes to party all night."

He smiled knowing that she had probably not been awake for any more than ten minutes herself.

She laughed. "And he's not the only one, is he?"

"Do you have a tropical suntan yet?" Doug quizzed.

"Not quite, but it's in progress."

"How's everyone?"

"Mama, Clarice and Julia went into town with the girls for a while. Emily said she wanted to be there when it was time for *siesta*. That's all she's talked about for most of the morning. Kely's sitting here sending air-kisses."

"Tell her I think that's very sweet, but she shouldn't be doing that kind of stuff in front of you." Doug joked.

"They're not for you, silly." She giggled and sighed. "I guess if you're not up yet then neither is Jerry."

"I doubt it. Shall I go check?"

He could hear Kely's disappointed sounds.

Again Sammy giggled. "Now it's daggers."

"I don't think Jerry will appreciate that." He smiled.

"I think they're aimed at you, dear." She giggled again, but Doug did not respond.

"So what have the two of you been doing?" She asked. The sound of her voice changed and Doug sensed it soften a bit with her new words.

"Well, mostly we got situated in our new digs yesterday. Gathered all of the info we'll need and are now working to get the final plan in shape for tomorrow."

"Doug, I'm worried for the two of you. Kely says that I shouldn't, but I can't help it." She confessed.

Anxiety flooded his awareness. How could he ever hope to answer her question when his own feelings about this situation were not yet sorted?

His heart ached to be with her.

He struggled for words, but none came easily. He took a long deep breath and whispered. "Sweetheart, I think you ought to listen to Kely. She's right on this."

"I know, Doug. Can you guys really do this job?"

"Well, it certainly appears to be *do-able*. When we finally take care of these three guys, it will be over."

"Doesn't this kind of stuff bother you?" She pined.

"Not half as much as being away from you does." He felt his level of anxiety expand again.

Instantly his memory was pulled to Catherine's deathbed. Then he had said about her—I should have married that woman. Now he knew that was what he also needed to do with Sammy.

She whispered. "Oh, Doug, that's so sweet. I miss you a lot more than that, too." In her thoughts she added, but you did not answer my question, hon.

Contemplating a moment, Doug took a deep breath and was finally ready to do it. "Sammy, I uh...."

Suddenly his angst stole his voice away. He stuttered, but words would not form to convey his feelings. His throat tightened as if to choke his life away.

"It's okay, Doug. I feel the same way about you."

Someone knocked several times on his bedroom door. "It's me, Doug." Jerry yelled from the hallway.

"Oops, someone's at the door. I've got to go."

Sammy kissed the phone several times before she spoke. "Okay, dear. I love you very much."

"Ditto. Bye."

Doug hung up the phone, grabbed for the sheet and yelled. "Come on in, Jerry."

"Hey, pal. Did you hear the phone ring earlier?"

"Yes. Sammy called accompanied by some hot woman, whose name I can't remember, but she was hoping to get the chance to make some moves on you."

Jerry grinned. "Did you tell her I was spoken for?"

"I did, but she said that didn't matter."

He shook his head with imaginary disgust.

"The three of you are totally and completely certifiable when you act like this. Did either of you happen to discuss how mama and the family were doing?"

"In the middle of all our laughter and cut-ups someone mentioned they were fine and missing us."

"Did that fiancée of mine mention anything?"

"Not really, just something about kisses and daggers. I didn't really understand it."

"You're as hopeless as those two women." He shook his head making sure it was properly exaggerated for the situation. "Get dressed and I'll fill you in on the latest behind the scene activities downstairs."

Jerry smiled enjoying the antics and left the room.

A few minutes later Doug appeared the dining room. The cook had prepared both of them a late breakfast and several plates of steaming food sat on the table.

Curt was munching on an apple and occasionally sipping on a nearby diet soft drink. Doug began eating. After a couple of minutes Jerry finished his meal and began discussing the new materials they had received.

"Overnight Curt gathered these photos of Harris' likely partners. By checking the people he usually hangs with he narrowed the list even more. Eventually he narrowed it to only these two officers."

Jerry tossed the photos on the table. Doug glanced at them briefly and through a surprised look nodded his recognition of both men.

Jerry smiled at the results and continued. "Pretty good, huh? Then he gathered background on them. First, we have Officer Darrell Allen Reynolds."

Doug looked briefly at Reynolds photo, straightened it and returned to his breakfast.

"Officer Reynolds, age 26, has been with the department for less than three years. He has had one *excessive force charge* made against him that was later dropped when he apologized to the victim and then paid $2,300 of the man's medical expenses.

"He's currently single, but has a steady girlfriend who is said to be a financial drain on his bank account.

"Next, we have Officer Frank Jose Garcia, age 37. He's been on the PD for six years and two more at a PD in the southwest. No charges have ever been made against him. He's divorced and still has regular contact with his three teenage children. There are reports of growing medical bills for one of them, so that might explain his looking to supplement his *dinero*."

"To me both of them sound like disasters just waiting for the right moment to come unglued." Doug said, as he pushed his empty plate aside for the cook.

"There's more info contained in here than we'll ever need to know on these guys. Curt, you've certainly outdone yourself."

He nodded an acceptance of the compliment, reached for his diet soft drink and took a long sip.

Doug inquired. "Okay, now what's been happening with Harris this morning?"

"Curt will fill you in on all that stuff. I'm going up to get a shower before the morning's gone. Afterwards I'll introduce you to someone who'll be very helpful to us."

Doug listened to the detailed explanation of Harris's movements, asked a couple of questions about the computer and then headed upstairs to take his own shower.

📖

An hour later both men sat in a corner booth of a newly refurbished downtown Los Angeles coffee shop. Most of its fifties décor was original. Tattered a bit in places, but very stylish today. Many of the staff were college students with part time jobs who seemed to enjoy wearing clothes from that recent period of history.

Doug and Jerry each sipped their coffee while awaiting their surprise guest. Doug faced the entrance.

Jerry spoke. "I think we've got an unacceptable situation if we can't handle the problem with Harris away from his home. I don't want his wife or family to become witnesses to anything we do, especially his untimely death."

Doug nodded. "Looks to me like you gangster-types also have hearts." He smiled.

"Touché. I guess I'd better learn from this not to call a jarhead a softy."

Doug added. "That's good. If you're really serious about moving away from those old ways rooted in the past you'll have to make some immediate changes like that."

Nodding, Jerry agreed. "I'm working on a plan to get his wife out of town, if any of that becomes necessary. Also, I've got another scheme to draw him and his partners back to that warehouse for a confrontation where we will be in control. You should be able to do some serious damage to them and their morale in less than a half hour."

"Won't that be risky?"

"Not really. Most people don't know that there is an

open structure of wooden trusses and beams throughout the attic with access panels leading to many of the rooms below. Once you get it figured out, you'll be all over them and they won't be able to keep track of you, much less catch you. How does that sound? It might even be fun."

His eyes seemed to sparkle at the suggestion.

"Much like climbing around the barn as kids, huh?"

Jerry looked pleased. "I think you'll enjoy this."

"No doubt. You know, I remember once I...."

Doug glanced to the side and into the face of a brand new uniformed LA police officer, standing next to his table. His face held his surprise.

Upon seeing Doug's expression Jerry's head jerked to see what had grabbed his attention.

"Oh, there you are. I was wondering if you'd be able to get away this morning. Doug, this is Officer Fabroni. He'll be aiding us with a very important little matter."

Doug stood and extended a hand. "I'm Doug Carlson."

After shaking hands he made room for Fabroni on his side of the booth. He was young and obviously a rookie.

Speaking with an immature voice that fell just short of being squeaky, Officer Fabroni asked. "Doug Carlson... hmmm, I seem to remember hearing that name last winter in the news. Did all of that mess finally get worked out?"

Doug nodded, but was not exactly clear about what mess he was talking about since most of his plight was never in the news and it involved things that a rookie would not usually be able to access.

A waitress approached and poured coffee for the newly arrived guest. Cautiously he sipped it.

Jerry completed the introduction. "Leroy is my Cousin

Antonio's boy. He's just getting started in his career. He's wanted to be a cop since he was this high, right?" Jerry grinned as he held his hand to the side measuring about forty inches from the floor.

Fabroni offered a big grin and nodded sheepishly.

"Leroy, we need some help from you that hopefully won't compromise your solid position with the PD. Do you know a Detective Harris in the West LA Precinct?"

He nodded and took another sip of his coffee.

"Well, we have a surprise for him and need your help getting it to his desk without anyone else knowing."

"If it's not illegal, I'll gladly help out."

📖

Twenty minutes later Wilson telephoned Townsen's office. "Sir, you're not going to believe this. A reliable snitch just phoned me from a downtown deli saying he had spotted Carlson talking to a rookie cop. He says they look pretty friendly."

"Was he able to overhear any of the conversation?"

"No, sir.... Hold on a moment. Something else is coming in." There was a pause.

"Sir, this report will blow your socks off. Preliminary reports say that Bruno Sebastino has retired and moved to some unknown little town in South America. Joseph Baldevino has replaced him as head of the local Mafia establishment. Plans for a formal ceremony are being made and it is expected to be held next Saturday evening."

"I'll be damned. I wonder how much Harris played in all of this? Make contact with Carlson. I want some detailed answers from him *pronto*."

📖

Fabroni stopped his patrol vehicle in the underground-parking garage of Harris' precinct. Carlson sat comfortably in his partner's seat.

Activity in the area was sparse.

He parked near the freight elevator.

"Normally you would need a visitors badge, but with an escort I hope we can avoid that."

Carlson carried three manila folders filled with blank sheets of paper making the stack about two inches thick. Harris was usually at lunch this time of day and the tail on him confirmed it to be true today.

His office was expected to be empty.

They took an elevator to the fourth floor where Fabroni navigated the corridors with ease.

Occasionally officers passed the two of them, smiled and offered a friendly nod.

Fabroni walked nonchalantly into the bright office. Six desks were arranged so as to provide little space for any other movement. An officer sat at one of the desks near the back of the room.

"Excuse me, sir. Which desk is Detective Harris'?"

With a brief glance he pointed to a desk along the wall. They approached it. A stack of papers sat on one side. Refuse from a hurried breakfast covered the other.

Doug laid the folders that he carried in the middle of the desk. He picked up a red pen and wrote a message to Harris on the first sheet of paper inside the top folder.

Fabroni inquired of the other detective. "When do you expect him back?"

The response came without him looking up. "Don't have any idea exactly. Probably very late in the day."

📖

Jerry gave the orders. "Hank, I need you and your guys to find a woman living in Santa Barbara by the name of Joanna May Peterson. She's the sister of Detective Harris' wife. Involve her in a minor accident so that she's injured slightly. Be gentle with her."

There was a pause while Jerry thought about it.

"Select a perp who'll be very sympathetic and stay with her as much as possible. I want her treated very well and don't forget to take care of all her medical expenses. I need it done by four this afternoon."

"No problem, sir. I can handle that."

Chapter Sixteen

Harris pulled into an aged dumpy looking hamburger joint with abundant parking on one side. He drove to the last space in the rear.

He saw mostly Hispanic clientele. Definitely not a place he would frequent. Too much grief happened in this area to make him feel comfortable.

Besides, it was Garcia's beat.

Reynolds parked his patrol vehicle next to Harris'.

They stood behind the cars and chatted about work until Garcia arrived. A young Mexican man sat in the rear seat of his patrol vehicle. He was probably the reason for their meeting, Harris thought.

After Garcia parked both men exited the vehicle.

"Gentlemen, this is Hector. He's a good guy and manages to hear a lot of what's said on the streets. He came to me about an hour ago saying that Baldevino wanted to see us this evening in that old warehouse."

Harris moved so that he towered menacingly over Hector with an attitude he reserved for anyone he did not like or who was not white.

"Is that right, boy?" He scowled at him and sprayed saliva on him.

Hector nodded and leaned against the trunk of the police cruiser. Harris maintained his uncomfortable stance and demeanor. Hector could not hide his growing fear.

"Who is Baldevino?"

Hector responded with his naturally poor English pronunciation. "He's new *Dun*. Not *Sabatini*, but *Balavino*."

Harris looked confused. He turned away feeling his frustration and muttered a racial slur under his breath.

Garcia moved forward to protect Hector.

Reynolds wisecracked. "Shall I just pop him, sir?"

Garcia took over.

"Knock it off, guys. He's trying to help us out, so cut the bullshit with him." He spoke to Hector in Spanish. After several sentences he turned to Harris.

"He thinks he's forgotten part of what he was suppose to tell us, but he does remember that we're to meet Baldevino in an old warehouse at eleven tonight."

"Which warehouse? Did he forget that too?"

Garcia translated the question into Spanish.

Hector responded. Garcia translated for him. "That's what he might have forgotten, but he thinks we're suppose to know which one."

📖

Jim and Marie had moved to Santa Barbara from Los Angeles two years after her auto accident. The mishap had also taken the life of one of their children, so moving to a new area made the recovery somewhat easier for them to handle. Jim's company gladly transferred him to aid them with Marie's recuperation.

Hank's call had come less than an hour ago and he was expected to arrive at their home at any moment. Others had already located Joanna Peterson and she was being tracked in a nearby shopping mall.

The horn of a red van honked.

Jim peeked through the curtains. He rushed to get Marie and struggled to push her non-motorized wheelchair toward the front sidewalk.

At the door they were met by Hank. He was overweight, but well dressed and very friendly.

"How you folks doing?"

He extended a moist slimy hand to Jim and then offered it to Marie. Pleasantries were exchanged.

"We've got a real tight schedule, folks, so if we can get moving I'd appreciate it."

One of his assistants in the van helped load Marie and her wheelchair. In eight minutes they turned into the parking lot at La Cumbra Plaza in northern Santa Barbara near State Street and Highway 101.

The driver stopped at the top of a landscaped ramp.

"We'll hop out here and get things setup."

Jim expressed his growing worry. "Are you sure this is the right thing for us to be doing?"

"Who knows? I'm only doing what I'm told just like you, right? We're setting up an accident to create a minor injury and that's it, right."

Briefly Hank walked away to make sure others were in their proper place before the show could get started.

He returned to Marie. "Okay, my dear. This is what's planned. The target will be brought out of that door by one of our security people. She's been told that her car has just been stolen and then quickly recovered right down there."

He pointed briefly to both locations.

"While she's talking to that man over there, Jim will accidentally lose control of your chair. As you speed toward them you'll scream like crazy. That's very important. At the last second he'll step aside and you'll collide only with her. There'll be someone behind her to aid with breaking the fall and hopefully stop both of you so that we can avoid everything but the intended injuries. That's not much to remember for two-grand, is it?"

Marie smiled. "What's her name?"

"I can't tell you that, but you'll know soon enough."

Her hand found Jim's.

She squeezed it and looked into his worried face. "Do you think this kind of thing is really okay?"

"I think it's suppose to be one of those things that is planned to produce a good outcome for everybody."

Through a faint smile of apprehension she whispered to calm his fears. "I sure hope so."

📖

Jerry met Fabroni's patrol vehicle several miles from the precinct. They stopped so that their drivers' doors were adjacent. Warmly Doug shook hands with Leroy and then moved to the van. After brief good-byes that promised the cousins would soon get together, they parted.

Jerry asked Doug. "How'd it go inside the precinct?"

"Not too bad. I left Harris a special message."

"Good. What'd it say?"

"Just a few words of appreciation between friends."

Jerry shook his head and turned the van at the next corner heading for their temporary home at #423.

📖

From ten feet away the security guard shouted. "Paging Joanna Peterson." Surprised at hearing her name she turned and cautiously raised her hand to get his attention.

The young man rushed toward her. "Mrs. Peterson?"

She nodded.

"Excuse me, Ma'am, but in the parking lot someone tried to steal your car. We caught them in the act and called your husband first. He's the one who told us you were probably still shopping. Can you come with me to check out the condition of your vehicle and see if anything has been stolen from it?"

Joanna was visibly shaken by the news.

She followed the guard at a fast pace.

Her long dark hair waved behind her. Being a little bit overweight caused her to breathe heavily after less than thirty seconds of exertion. Her confusion was high. She became worried and ran to stay abreast with the man.

Shortly a second guard joined them and immediately offered to carry her packages. They exited the mall in a southerly direction and immediately moved east stopping halfway down a long, well-landscaped ramp.

Her car was parked at the curb.

The passenger door was open.

Another guard sat in the driver's seat. A security vehicle with an activated light bar sat nearby with a suspect locked in the rear seat.

Joanna offered a sigh of relief upon surveying the scene. She scanned the back seat of her car for her earlier packages. They were still there.

To her the car looked fine.

Her state of worry began to recede.

They stopped two feet behind her car and turned to finish the report. One guard holding an open report book was uphill with the sun at his back.

The other was to her right.

Joanna looked into the sun and squinted.

She fumbled in her purse for a pair of sunglasses.

In the distance someone screamed.

Both guards knew what to expect, but held their positions. One of them counted as he turned his head toward the scream. An out of control wheelchair approached. A frantic man ran after it. The guard finished his count and jumped quickly out of the way.

One of the wheelchair's foot-supports impacted Joanna's left shin. Marie's body flew into Joanna's.

The crash was solid.

A second guard jumped behind Joanna to assist with the coming fall. Instantly three people were on the ground with an overturned wheelchair resting on its side.

Joanna cried from the sharp pain.

Marie nursed several scrapes and then cried for Joanna. Jim's exasperation was evident as he tried to explain his misfortune to one of the guards.

Another guard called 911.

In twenty minutes Joanna would discover that her left leg had been fractured in the mishap.

📖

Harris answered his cellular phone. "Yeah."

"It's me, honey." Pamela responded.

"Hi. I can't talk long."

"I just had a frantic call from Joanna. She's been hurt. Something about her car being stolen at the mall and she ended up with a broken leg."

"Was she assaulted?"

"I don't think so. Frankly her story didn't make a lot of sense on the phone. If you don't mind I'd like to drive up and visit with her and Bob for the weekend. Maybe you can come up and join us tomorrow?"

"That's okay, but why don't you go on up by yourself and help her out. I'll visit with them another time."

"You sure you don't mind if I go up alone?"

"It's fine. I'll just have some of the guys over for a while tomorrow night and play some cards."

"If you're sure, then I'll leave as soon as I can pack a few things and get on the road."

"Okay, have a good time."

He turned off the phone and parked in front of the precinct. He planned to rush inside and stay just long enough to check through his afternoon messages.

Virgil still sat at his desk. He looked up.

"Hey, Jason. How goes it?"

"Busy day. How about you?"

"Yep, same old shit for me everyday." He leaned back in his worn office chair.

Harris slid into his chair. "What's this?"

Virgil stretched to see what he was talking about. "Oh, that. A rookie dropped that off during lunch."

Harris opened the top folder. In big red letters a neatly printed note read:

BANG, BANG. YOU'RE DEAD.

Chapter Seventeen

Harris walked through the door of *The Watering Hole*. In the distance he could see that Reynolds and Garcia had already arrived and probably conned someone out of the corner booth. He stopped at the bar.

"Pete, how about a double *JD on the rocks*?"

He smiled at the order. "That kind of a day, huh?"

Harris nodded. "Those guys drinking their usual?"

Pete tilted his head to the side a bit and looked toward the booth. "Sure looks like it."

"When this is gone send me more of the same thing."

"You got it, Jason."

Harris walked to the quiet booth.

Reynolds and Garcia munched on wings and spuds. He slid onto the seat. Both men looked at him, but neither spoke. Harris unfastened his holster with its revolver and plunked it on the table.

The men stopped eating and stared at him. Their curious looks lingered until Harris spoke.

"What?" He exclaimed.

Reynolds hastily swallowed his food and spoke to Harris. "What's going on here?"

Garcia nodded.

The food was forgotten.

Tossing the folded sheet of paper on the table Harris said with disgust in his voice. "Some fucking joker paid me a visit this afternoon."

Garcia picked it up and glanced at the writing.

"Holy Mother of Jesus." He said as he passed it to Reynolds and made the sign of the cross.

Reynolds gasped. "Oh, shit. I knew something like this was going to happening."

Several cops in nearby booths looked toward them.

"Keep your voice down, Reynolds. I don't want this going public." Harris cautioned.

Getting over his shock Garcia added. "Is this for real?"

"I'm not sure, but if it is we're in deep trouble."

Reynolds uttered. "What are you planning to do?"

"We're keeping that meeting this evening with Mr. Baldevino, so we don't look like a bunch of weenies."

📖

Friday night reservations at *The Sandalwood Café and Restaurant* were often unattainable, but it was Jerry's favorite eatery. The right connections, a discreet phone call and $200 would move anyone to the top of the list whenever they walked through the front door.

He and Doug relaxed in the crowded lower gardens overlooking the Pacific Ocean with its light roar. Their dinner had just arrived. The sun would be out of sight shortly. Doug's mind focused on the sunset's colors.

"Earlier the tail on Harris reported that he had left his office in such a hurry that he almost caused two accidents. He was at that police dive just long enough to get his partners all riled up. They left there in a hurry too." Jerry said.

"Sounds like we put the fear of God into them."

"I think you're right. By the way, Harris' wife made plans with him late this afternoon to spend the weekend in Santa Barbara tending to her injured sister." Jerry added in a matter of fact tone.

With wide eyes Doug asked. "You didn't hurt that unfortunate woman did you?"

"Well…."

"No, tell me you didn't do anything like that?"

"This was so expertly done that she doesn't have a clue it wasn't a real accident. As a matter of fact she and her husband even invited the unfortunate woman who took the spill with her to dinner this evening. So don't ever underestimate the highly persuasive power of groveling, especially if a woman is the one doing it."

"That's disgusting, Jerry."

"No, it's not! That's exactly how a lot of things are getting done in today's complicated world."

📖

By six o'clock Harris and his men acted as though they were on a holy mission. They cruised every mob joint they could remember and rousted anyone who would not say exactly what they wanted to hear.

They were having little success.

The bouncers in two clubs made immediate phone reports to their local precinct knowing that Harris and his men would leave when confronted by officers that the mob had already bought and paid for.

They had found absolutely nothing until confronting Oscar, the person who had passed the bait along to Hector earlier in the day. Of course he was happy to talk to them.

His spoken English was much better than Hector's, but he tried very hard to mispronounce as many words as he could in order to stall and complicate the situation. Upsetting his tormentors as much as he could was a part of this assignment that he really enjoyed.

With threats of being arrested Harris persuaded him into a back room. All three men faced him as a group in a final showdown of wills.

Harris led the charge. "So give me the skinny on Sebastino and don't leave anything out, if you know what's good for you."

"You mean Bruno Sebastino, right?" Oscar toyed.

"Of course, you dumb-ass."

Oscar smiled. He liked having these greedy pigs begging him for info, but thinking they were in control of another dumb Mexican. "I heard he got retired and moved to somewhere in South America. Lima, Peru, I think."

Oscar smiled since he had just made up the Peru bit.

"So he's in good health and will enjoy his long awaited and much deserved retirement?" Harris asked.

Oscar's tone and accommodating smile were convincing. "Oh yeah, he had a nasty fall earlier in the week, I think, but he's recovered from it. Doing real good, I hear."

Harris' and his men looked puzzled, but did not divulge that they knew otherwise.

"Is there a man named Joseph Baldevino in your organization?"

"Oh yeah, he's the man Mr. Sebastino asked to take over for him here in LA. I hear they're really tight, I think. You know what I mean, right?" He crossed his fingers and held them out to demonstrate how close they were.

"Would you excuse us for a moment?" Harris needed to sort out this wild story.

The three men stepped to the side.

Oscar responded as they walked away. "Sure man. Take your time. I always cooperate with the law."

Whispering, Reynolds said. "This is a crock of bullshit. I pumped enough lead into those guys to kill fifty of them. There's no retirement for him except for a long stay in the dirt farm."

Garcia added his opinion. "What do you make of the fact that this is the second person to tell us the same story? I kind of believe him."

"I don't like it. This is making me crazy."

Then Harris spoke up. "What are the chances that Bruno might have survived all those bullets?"

Reynolds did not hesitate. "I say it's slim and none. This guy is fucking with us. I can see it in his face."

"And why would he do that? He doesn't know you from any other cop, does he?"

"No, but I tell you this is some weird shit happening. I don't like it. Let's put a gun to this guys head and see if that changes his tune to something more believable."

Harris raised his voice. "Get a grip, Reynolds. This guy has no reason to lie. Garcia's right, he doesn't know you from a stinking fence post."

Harris paused. Reynolds shook his head in disbelief.

"Okay, guys. What do we do with this piece of shit story?" Harris asked.

Garcia answered. "Let's see if this guy knows why Baldevino wants to meet with us. That's a start."

Harris nodded, turned toward Oscar and asked. "Have you heard any scuttlebutt about why Baldevino is all set to meet with some LA cops this evening?"

"Sure, I heard it's some bad police-dude named Harris. That's you, right?"

Harris nodded.

Oscar continued. "I thought so, why else would you be asking me so many questions about this stuff?"

"So, Baldevino expects to meet me and my officers in that old warehouse on Coleman Street tonight, right?"

"Yes, that's what he said." Oscar nodded.

"Did he say why?"

"Sure, you wanted to get some steady work from Mr. Sebastino, right?" Harris nodded again. "Well, Mr. Baldevino says he would like to have some legal muscle to work for him too, I think."

Harris was now ready to leave. "Oscar, you're giving all this to me straight, right?"

Oscar nodded and smiled broadly.

"If not, I'm coming back to cut your tongue out."

Oscar nodded several more times.

Harris turned and walked away. After a prolonged

glare from Reynolds, the others followed him.

As they walked out the door, Oscar grinned.

📖

At 10:17 p.m. Doug and Jerry had finished their dinner and were leaving the restaurant.

A light ocean breeze caressed the balmy evening. Both men were full of food and conversation, but a busy night lay ahead for both of them. Nearing the van a man's voice called out from the darkness. "Excuse me, Mr. Carlson."

Pausing, they turned to face the voice. Jerry's hand slipped inside his coat and around the grip of a .38 caliber Smith & Wesson snub-nose revolver he was licensed to carry. Instinctively his thumb popped the snap and pulled back its silent trigger.

The pleasant man spoke. "I'm Agent Wilson. I work with Otis Townsen. Do you remember him?"

"Yes, and I also remember you, too, Agent Wilson." Doug offered his hand and they shook. He turned to Jerry. "This is Bruno Sebastino's son, Jerry."

"It's a pleasure, Mr. Sebastino." They shook, then Wilson turned back toward Doug with his comment.

"Townsen has a few questions for you."

"Well, he can save them for another time when it's not so late. I'm about to go home for the evening."

Doug yawned to make his point.

"Okay, do you mind if I ask a few questions now?"

"Not as long as we get on with it."

"Fair enough. Has anything happened between you and Detective Jason Harris of the LAPD?"

"I'm sorry, but I don't think I know him." He shook his head and looked to Jerry for recognition of the name.

Wilson knew it was a lie, but continued his questioning. "Where have you been for the past few days?"

"I was out of town visiting with my girlfriend and her family. I'm thinking of popping the big question and thought it would be smart to meet with them first."

Jerry's eyes focused on Doug. He silently praised him for such a convincing lie.

"And where would that be, sir?"

"They live in Tucson. I thought you guys already had all that stuff on file for me and my girlfriend."

Agent Wilson glanced briefly at Jerry. "No, sir. We don't keep that kind of info on citizens any longer. Mr. Sebastino, where is your father?"

At first Jerry looked stunned. "Well, sir... to tell you the truth he's out of the country and I'm not exactly sure where he's actually staying this evening."

"And just one last question, gentlemen. Do either of you know who Joseph Baldevino is?"

Doug shook his head.

Jerry responded. "No, sir. I don't."

Wilson thanked them, excused himself and exited toward his vehicle.

A chill in the air suddenly developed.

As they climbed into the van, Doug spoke. "I'm sure the feds know something has happened, but they're obviously missing some great big pieces of it."

They chuckled.

📖

They arrived at the warehouse with plenty of time for Jerry to give Doug a lengthy detailed tour before anyone else was scheduled to arrive. First, he identified where the major attic entrances and exits were located, then a number of unusual ways to move through the various sections. Many rooms had access panels hidden in closets, storage rooms, vents or bathrooms. Doug liked the layout for the confusion it would create for the uninformed.

After ten minutes Jerry suggested that Doug go exploring on his own. He jumped at the chance.

A few minutes later Doug found a roof access door and two alcoves that would provide nice hiding places, if necessary. Within fifteen minutes he had explored most of the cavernous space and then dropped back to the floor in front of Jerry from the same ceiling opening he had earlier disappeared through.

Jerry was not surprised to see him. "A pretty nice place to get lost in, isn't it?" He smiled widely.

Doug returned the smile, thinking that it had been fun. "It sure is. Climbing around some of those dark spaces took me back quite a few years."

"Well, it's 10:38. I'd better get out of here before your party gets started. I'd hate to spoil it. I hope you didn't forget anything that you'll need. By the way there is a rented blue Escort waiting for you two blocks west of here on Hopkins Drive. The ignition key is hidden in a magnetic box placed behind the driver's rear wheel."

Doug pulled on dark leather gloves and climbed back up into the attic.

"Hey, pal, before you split can you pass that bag up?"

Chapter Eighteen

Harris, Reynolds and Garcia had just finished their dinner at a fast-food restaurant on Clemsone Street. Harris hated fish and chips, but both the others loved them and it was too late to make plans for anything else. Harris ate the chips and grumbled about the fish.

Garcia asked him. "Exactly how does it work?"

Harris acted annoyed. "How clear can it be? You keep them happy by supplying little pieces of info about pending busts and other kinds of legal stuff like that."

Reynolds added. "Haven't you ever felt like you were betraying your fellow officers by doing that?"

"No. If it ever came to a situation like that I'd tell those mob creeps I didn't have access to the data they wanted. How are they ever going to know otherwise?"

"What if they have someone else on the payroll who is willing to give them *what you say* you can't get?"

"Well, I guess he's the joker who betrays fellow officers, not me. You guys are making this way too hard."

Garcia asked again. "And then somebody just delivers an envelope of money to you each month?"

"That's how it works, sport." Harris resigned himself to answering these kinds of questions. He thought about how a few extra dollars had made a big difference for him in how well he lived and was finally able to get some of the finer things that he and Pamela wanted in life.

Reynolds bragged. "And, Celeste won't be getting a single dime of this money if I can help it."

They all looked at him.

Harris shook his head and smiled as they left the restaurant. Reynolds was such a talker he thought. He knew that was all it was.

They headed to their cars.

Garcia climbed in the front seat to ride with Harris.

📖

Townsen was almost asleep when his phone rang. The streetlight on the corner cast a yellowish glow over his bedroom. His wife did not stir.

He picked it up and whispered. "Hello."

"I'm sorry to bother you at this time of night, sir, but I just spoke to Carlson and Sebastino's kid."

"Did they give you anything on Harris?"

"Not really, it was just like meeting two choirboys out for dinner and now heading home. Oh, they were convincing, but after tailing them most of the afternoon I was not buying into most of what they told me."

"Where are they now?"

Wilson looked briefly at his watch.

"Sebastino's probably running the show from that mob safe house by now. Earlier they picked up a black sports bag at Carlson's home and then Sebastino dropped Carlson off at the Coleman Street warehouse. He's still here."

"What was in the bag?"

"I don't know. The way they tossed it around it could have been dirty gym clothes or some other stuff like that."

"Could it have contained weapons?"

"It may have, but I couldn't ascertain that for sure."

"Do you think this situation is heading towards a replay of the fireworks we saw last year?"

Wilson paused for a moment. "Good observation, sir. I hadn't thought of that, but you could be right."

Townsen wondered about the options. His silence lingered on what Carlson had already proven himself capable of doing. His thoughts ended with a big grin.

Agent Wilson interrupted. "Sir, what's the plan?"

"I've got a hunch, Wilson. Stick close to Carlson, but stay out of his way if you can. Keep him in sight and help him out *only* as a last resort."

"Are you sure about this, sir?"

"Didn't you say you trusted Carlson over Harris?"

"Yes, sir. I did."

"Well."

📖

His killing hardware had been kept in the black bag and it was now at his side. It was 10:45 and none of Har-

ris' men had arrived yet. Earlier in the day Doug had retrieved the bag and its deadly contents from its hiding
place. It would be useful to him again this evening.

He waited in the attic near the entrance.

Musty air surrounded him. Occasionally he heard paw
steps of scampering rodents. Years of accumulated dust
and debris soiled his gloves, face and clothing. His mind
wandered to Sammy, then to Catherine.

He fought to stay focused in the moment.

Suddenly Doug heard the sound of automobile engines,
lots of them. He was surprised and wondered how the plan
might have changed. He moved to a crack in the wall to
view the area in front of the warehouse.

He gasped at what he saw.

There were three patrol vehicles with full flashing
lights, four detective vehicles and a paneled vehicle much
like what a swat team might use.

He cringed. It seemed the situation was now completely out of control before it had begun.

📖

Harris exited his vehicle.

At the very last moment he decided to take no chances.
Meeting with anyone, especially the mob, on equal terms
was not his usual style. Without an advantage of some sort
he could not easily ensure the outcome he sought.

He had ordered a couple of escort vehicles to assure
there would be no foul play from anyone before hand. Although he wanted the mob's money for what he considered
to be useless information, he did not trust any private in-

teractions he might have with them.

He looked around. The warehouse looked deserted.

He was finally pleased. Getting here first held advantages, he thought.

Of the thirteen officers present most were already being paid regularly by the local mob or else soon hoped to be. That was just one part of Harris' plan.

His recent bloody demonstration of personal initiative had been designed to make him and his proposal more valuable, not exactly a shakedown, but close. He had no way of knowing that instead of that it marked him as a loose cannon, a dangerous position to be in when associated so closely with the Mafia.

Everyone converged on Harris' position. He paused briefly as they gathered around him.

"Gentlemen, we have a somewhat delicate situation to deal with here. I want this building secured in five minutes then I want the black and whites gone. Every breathing thing goes to the paddy wagon, then I want it gone ASAP.

"Those of you who remain behind will be posted in various locations to control access to the warehouse. Absolutely no one comes out or goes in without me knowing about it before hand. Understood?"

There were a number of nods. Harris looked over the men's faces. "Any questions?"

One of the uniformed officers spoke in an unsure voice. "Sir, those of us who have to leave early will still be on *the hiring list*, right?"

"Yes."

He paused to await others. None were asked.

"Okay, you all know what to do."

Doug smiled having listened to Harris' *big talk* and then chuckled about Harris finding out that he was actually the one being conned this time. Headlights lit the front of the warehouse. Strands of light illuminated his face.

He paid close attention to his targets.

Harris wore a dark colored blazer. Reynolds wore a windbreaker, jeans and cowboy boots. Garcia wore a leather bomber jacket and dark pants.

Doug thought, after dealing with Mr. C's goons last year, these guys looked like little more than child's play.

Uniformed and plain-clothes officers ran to secure the building. Many had withdrawn their side arms.

Turning Doug leaned against the wall. He sighed.

Five minutes ought to be more than enough time to get their plan fully situated. That ought to be more than enough time for them.

His mind wandered to Catherine. Memories of good times flooded his face and warmed his heart.

He knew he had been right earlier when he suggested that he should have married her. The signs were all around him, her devotion and frequent displays of affection, her support and constant encouragement. Her display of love often brought special feelings that nearly burst his heart.

How could I have not seen them and acted to accept their wonderful implication?

He had paid many times for those personal omissions with additional failed words, restless dreams and an empty heart. *Could things now be different with Sammy?*

His thoughts turned to her.

Feelings of near emotional perfection swept over him. She had suffered loss too, yet had slowly recovered and surrendered herself again to him.

Why could he not do the same for her? All the easy answers eluded him. Uncertainty encircled his thoughts.

Someone stirred in the room below jarring him back to the moment. Heavy footsteps ascended the stairs leading to his location above that room.

His heart froze.

His keen eyes were now accustomed to the murkiness. Tiny threads of light pierced the darkness and painted airborne dust near the closed access door.

He held his breath and silently moved toward it while unsheathing a ten-inch razor sharp blade. He stepped behind the panel as it rose. His heartbeat increased until it sounded like thunder.

The hi-powered beam from a police flashlight flooded his prior location. He watched it scour the darkness for any possible intruder.

A leather-clad arm pushed against the panel.

Doug's heart raced but soon stilled. This would be his first chance for payback.

He held his breath and waited.

The panel reached a certain point and locked in the up position. Finally, it was time for him to act.

Grabbing Garcia's left arm, Doug lunged with the knife. Instantly his knife sliced deep into soft flesh. Turning the blade quickly, he added another long slicing motion as he withdrew the blade.

He knew that was more than enough to kill any man.

The flashlight trembled but never slipped from Garcia's hand. The struggle was short. That kind of trauma coupled with a massive blood loss usually ended a life in mere seconds. Doug knew it was over after several futile gasps for air from Garcia.

He eased the body to the floor.

Blood flowed freely. He needed to act fast.

The mess it had already created would be a problem. His anxiety surged wondering if anyone else was in the room below and might have seen or heard him.

He dragged the body toward a nearby air-conditioning unit. He hoped that would fix things for a while.

Rummaging through his black bag, Doug found a hand towel. Hastily he wiped the blood splatter from the stairs and from around the panel opening.

In the dimly lit area that would be enough, he thought and was pleased that no one else had seen the bloody event. He flung the now dripping towel toward Garcia and then gently closed the heavy panel.

Doug wiped his hands on his jeans then moved toward an open area of the attic with a direct view into the main warehouse space. It was open all the way to the rear wall.

Harris and his men gathered on the West Side of the building. They milled about waiting for a visitor that Doug knew would not arrive. Their hopes of earning extra cash that evening would never materialize.

Remaining in the shadows, Doug easily picked out Reynolds standing casually next to Harris. He looked at his watch. It was 11:24.

He worried that it would not be long before someone in the group suggested that it was a setup and that Baldevino was not coming.

He had to make something else happen before that.

Doug's mind sought an appropriate action from among the alternatives, but none seemed to be right.

He needed a diversion that would separate them into smaller groups where he hoped for the chance to get one of his targets alone for a minute.

He searched his bag to find a four-foot piece of rope that he quickly wound into the shape of a ball, secured the ends and tossed it toward the back side of the warehouse.

It hit the wall, bounced several times, then fell to the concrete with a noticeable thud. It was clear that everyone had heard the sound.

Most looked up to see where it had originated. Two officers drew their weapons and moved cautiously toward the rolling object.

Immediately Harris shouted. "Find out who the hell is hiding up there. I want him standing in front of me to answer questions, now!"

The men scrambled.

Still in the shadows Doug kept his eyes glued to Reynolds who exited from view in an easterly direction. Doug also went in that direction trying to be as quiet as possible.

Remembering there were no stairs into the rooms in this area, he would have to drop to the floor in one of several places. He neared the first hatch and peeked.

The room was empty, but this was too close to the main warehouse. He decided to go all the way to the last room and exit there.

Twenty seconds later he pried at the hatch and it moved enough for him to peek inside.

He saw the room was empty. He dropped his bag.

There was a muted thud and he followed it to the floor. Immediately he was on his feet ready to fight, but no one had heard the stirrings.

He opened a window and dropped his bag into the weeds and shadows next to the wall. He kept the knife and a .45 caliber semiautomatic pistol tucked loosely into his waistband.

Quietly he moved to the door and listened.

At times like this one's imagination can play tricks.

Doug was positive someone was listening on the other side of the door. He held his breath as if to divine their presence. His ear lightly touched the door, nothing.

It was a strange feeling, but it would not leave him.

The doorknob moved slightly.

He stepped aside to make room for the door to open. His heartbeat accelerated. His breath slowed.

When the door was open six inches, he grabbed it and pulled with all of his strength.

A young detective flipped headlong into the room.

Since it was not Reynolds, Doug did not want to kill him. Instead he kicked the man hard in the side then kicked him in the groin. While the man was doubled-up with his pain, Doug grabbed the man's handcuffs and locked his hands loosely behind him.

As the man's senses returned, Doug stooped in front of him. Pain still contorted the man's mouth. When the detective first opened his eyes, they met Doug's.

Fear flushed the young man's face.

Doug grasped the knife firmly. Leaning closer to the man, he whispered his orders. "Play dead for a while. Remember my face or make any sound, I'll come back and cut you up… more than you'll want to think about."

The man closed his eyes and rolled over on the floor.

Cautiously Doug moved into the hallway.

He listened briefly and moved toward the next room.

As Doug slowly approached the door to his left, Reynolds walked out of it and muttered. "What the…."

Reflexively Doug slammed the edge of the pistol into his face. Blood splattered from his broken nose and lip.

Reynolds grabbed Doug by his shoulders, spun him with forceful energy then pushed him hard into the wall. The pistol fell to the floor.

Reynolds dove for it.

Drawing his knife Doug fell on Reynolds and stabbed him in the right shoulder. Blood flowed quickly and easily from the long gash.

Reynolds reached the pistol, but failed to grasp it.

Doug stabbed him again.

Reynolds placed his hand over the wound, but blood seemed to flow even quicker. He rolled to get out of Doug's way and they came face to face again.

Each man grabbed the other's wrist.

They rolled several more times. These new exertions brought groans and grimaces from both men.

Reynolds' hand broke free and awkwardly grabbed the pistol. Instantly Doug had his hand on the gun too.

The test of strength had begun.

Reynolds struggled to slide his index finger into the trigger housing. Doug resisted the attempted movement, then tried to shift their weight away from his knife-wielding hand.

Each man endured.

Finally Doug rolled so that the knife was raised high in the air. With all his energy he pressed it toward Reynolds' face, harder and harder he pushed, then in an instant he reversed his energy.

He broke Reynolds' grip.

With a quick lunge he forced the knife between two of Reynolds' ribs and upwards into his heart. Doug pulled away a bit and thrust the knife hard and deep into the soft stomach area.

The resistance from Reynolds halted. He was not dead, but he soon would be.

Breathing heavily, Doug wiped the blade on Reynolds' pants and headed for the open window where his bag was hidden. With two of his targets dead, safety was now his major concern.

As he moved through the room where the young detective had been handcuffed, there was no hint from him of any recognition or movement.

Doug climbed though the open window and moved cautiously toward the front of the warehouse.

📖

Several men reported back to Harris after they found nothing. He swore, shook his head and walked hurriedly after Reynolds. He was ready to call everything off and get the hell out of there before anything else could happen.

Two of his men followed close behind him.

They went down the first hallway checking inside of each room as they moved. When they turned the first corner the sight of seeing Reynolds' body face down in a pool of blood caused Harris to stop in his tracks.

Surprise wrenched his gut and flung his mouth ajar.

The others moved forward to inspect the limp body.

Harris turned to walk away, mumbling. "He was afraid something like that would happen."

📖

In front of the main warehouse door another officer had been posted. Endlessly he strolled back and forth guarding the silent entrance.

As the man turned back toward the door, Doug broke into a sprint. Within seconds he was airborne with both of his feet aimed to impact the policeman squarely in the middle of his back.

The officer flew forward and slid helplessly to the ground. Doug landed with all of his weight coming to rest on top of the man.

The officer scrambled to regain control but could not. In spite of the commotion no one appeared to aid him.

Immediately Doug grabbed the man's hands and pulled them painfully tight behind him.

Breathing hard, Doug leaned toward the man's ear and whispered. "You yell, I break'em."

The man relaxed a little.

Searching the man, Doug found a pistol and shoved it into his own belt. He whispered again. "I don't plan to hurt you, so be cool, okay?"

He found the man's cuffs and secured his hands behind him. The man offered no resistance. He lifted and pointed the officer toward the corner of the building.

At Doug's insistence they shuffled toward the side of the building and as they entered the darkness, Doug spoke to the man. "Do I have to hit you to keep you quiet?"

The officer whispered. "I think you'd better hit me."

Using the man's gun Doug hit him in the side of the neck then tossed it beside him on the ground.

Staying in the shadows Doug moved to the street.

As he passed Harris' car, he kicked the passenger door. Twenty feet later his frustration got the better of him and he turned toward it, withdrew his .45 and fired four shots into the gas tank.

It exploded instantly like lightning into a giant ball of red and yellow flame.

Chapter Nineteen

The twenty-minute drive to #423 seemed to take little more than five. After finding the car that had been stashed for him he stopped briefly to phone Jerry with news of what had just happened.

Doug's adrenaline high had already dissipated.

It was 12:26 a.m. He felt sleepy and tried to fight the yawns as they now arrived more frequently, but the night would not be over for hours.

When he pulled into the driveway of #423 his breakfast had already been prepared and awaited him.

Jerry was in a jubilant mood, anxious to hear what had happened while they ate. Doug recounted the story with all of the gory details.

Curt was half-asleep and sat slouched in front of his computer terminal with another diet soft drink, his apparent beverage of choice for all occasions. An oven-fresh fruit pastry would be his breakfast for that day.

A police scanner flashed and sputtered its reports near him. Intermittent barely audible broadcasts broke the low murmur in the room.

All were surprised that Harris had not yet reported the death of two of his men. Jokes about his motives came from each man at the table.

Curt grinned at the spectacle.

Laughter from Jerry and Curt filled the dining room and dominated the next twenty-five minutes. Doug's final comment ended their frolic. "You know, I have to go back and finish this job tonight."

Surprise found each face.

Jerry paused a moment then finally acknowledged it.

"Yeah, I guess you're right."

📖

The explosion of Harris' car was the last straw.

He was stunned and his men were demoralized. In less than an hour two of *Los Angeles' finest* had died at the hands of an unseen, avenging enemy.

Both men had struggled within feet of other officers, yet nothing had been seen or heard from either of them.

Angry men scrambled to move their vehicles away from the roaring fire. In this part of town such fires often went unreported. That might be the only break of the evening for Harris and his men.

The search for Garcia's body took another ten minutes. Both corpses now lay just outside the front door.

Since they found Reynolds' body, Harris had sought

explanations for what had just happened. Eventually he knew someone would have to explain these deaths. As the senior officer, they would probably expect an accounting from him first. Currently he was at a loss for suitable words, but to keep his job they could not be the truth.

Likewise, none of the other men wanted any attention on them until they were better prepared to answer the probing questions publicly. A number of younger officers decided to leave, telling Harris that they had changed their minds about working so closely for the mob. Reluctantly he let them go, promising to keep their names out of any reports he might eventually have to make.

The remaining three had been close friends for decades and they would stick with him regardless of the circumstances. Barney, Michael and Sam formed a circle with Harris to help him sort the consequences.

Mostly consumed, Harris's car was now an empty fuming shell. Sam uttered what they all were feeling. "Jason, this is *all fucked up*."

Barney nodded.

Michael suggested. "I think you might have to kiss that shield of yours goodbye, Jason."

"Yeah, how long till you can retire?" Sam asked.

Harris responded. "Just three years and then a month or so, but you're probably right, it's over now."

Several grimaced. Sam shook his head and then turned briefly as he swore.

Barney finally spoke up. "Maybe not."

All eyes focused on him for the solution.

"Who knows we're even here?" He motioned questioningly with his hands.

Someone barked. "Only about ten other officers and who knows how many Mafia creeps."

"And I ask again who's going to contradict us?"

Sam's face lit up as he joined him. "Yeah, each of those officers was here for the same reason as us. What would they possibly say?"

"Right, and who would believe those dope-headed low-life creeps working for Baldevino?" Barney added.

"Come on, guy. You're not going there, are you?" Michael blurted in his discomfort.

"Hey, those two guys are already dead. Why do we have to tell others that we were here, too?"

Michael turned to Harris. "You need to stop this, Jason. Together, we can all take the heat on this. What's the overall pain of a fine when it comes to respect for the body of a fallen officer?" He pointed to Reynolds and Garcia.

Harris shook his head.

"This bitter-sweet approach does avoid many embarrassing questions. After all, someone else killed them. Why should any of us have to pay for it?"

Upset gripped Michael. He took several steps before he turned. "Come on, guys. It's just not right. They've been our friends for years. They deserve decent funerals and much better treatment than this."

Barney continued with the scheme. "Look, the longer we wait the more chance there is of us being busted. Let's do it now or just go back to the precinct and face the music." He began walking toward his car and stopped. "No, this is not the time to fold. I say, do it."

Harris agreed quickly. "Okay, I'm in."

They all looked at Michael. He shook his head, but

gave up and relented. "Just one thing, fellows, promise me you'll never do something like this to me."

During the next five minutes they rearranged the scene. Reynolds' car was parked in the warehouse near a wooden section that they hoped would ignite and burn easily. His body was placed behind the wheel with Garcia sitting next to him. The car was doused with gasoline and a trail was poured leading toward the smoldering ruins of Harris' car.

When they were ready to leave, Barney tossed a gasoline-filled beer bottle toward the end of the flammable trail. The bottle broke on the concrete curb and its content spread to fill the gap.

The added gush of gasoline burst into flames.

The men sped off.

As the fire spread over the surface of the volatile gasoline, it found the prepared trail leading into the warehouse. Flames rippled easily along it.

The fifty-five feet of gasoline soaked earth took less than a minute to ignite.

Within seconds of that Reynolds' car exploded.

Five minutes later an anonymous phone call was made from a phone booth reporting the raging fire.

📖

Curt turned from his scanner. "Mr. Sebastino, isn't that warehouse we've been talking about on Coleman Street?"

"Yes." Jerry responded.

"Police and fire units are being dispatched there as we speak. Looks like somebody just torched it and now it's totally engulfed in flames."

Jerry asked. "Could you find out if that was done by anyone working for us?"

Curt reached for the phone.

Doug chuckled and joined them. "Looks like the heat's only getting started for Harris."

Jerry laughed. "I doubt if Harris has a clue about what he has started. Papa didn't think he was much more than a jerk, red-neck with a badge and a perpetual hard-on to get more money anyway he could."

Curt interrupted. "Excuse me, Mr. Sebastino, but that fire was started by someone else. The only people we have in that area is the tail on Harris."

"Okay. Where exactly is he now?"

"Let's see. At 12:42 he and three of his buddies stopped at a liquor store and spent $284 on primo booze and snacks. It looks to me like getting falling-down drunk is now on their early morning agenda."

With raised eyebrows Jerry looked toward Doug. They both chuckled.

📖

Sam and Michael sat at the breakfast bar. Barney had pulled a chair from the table, turned it around and straddled it like a cowboy would a horse.

Harris was busy preparing two frozen pizzas.

Chips, salsa and nuts were already being devoured. The enjoyment of fine Tennessee whisky and pricey Caribbean rum had begun too. The serving dishes were out and conveniently placed.

The scene had all the elegance of a feeding frenzy after

a long night of friendly poker. They howled with laughter at an off-color joke told by Barney.

Unfortunately their upbeat mood hid a number of unanswered questions. All knew that alcohol could mask them, but not resolve them. These men knew that inattention usually made things worse, but that soul searching would have to come sometime later, maybe never.

A pleasant aroma filled the room. The jokes became raunchier. Harris peeked at the pizza and signaled with four fingers when they could be eaten. Much of the upset from earlier in the evening had been easily forgotten after only a few drinks.

The phone rang.

Sam grabbed it. "Hello."

There was hesitation. Pamela searched to remember the name behind the man's voice. "Sam, it that you?"

"Certainly, darling. You're missing some fine moments here." Laughter broke in the background.

She giggled through her drowsiness. "I know. How's Judy? Did you leave her at home again this evening?"

"Yeah. One of the granddaughters is staying over for the weekend and she wouldn't go out."

"That's where you should be, too." She scolded.

"Well, all those kids movies they watch puts me to sleep, so I'm here protecting my sanity."

"That sounds pretty unlikely coming from you. Is that drunken husband of mine anywhere near the phone?" She asked through a sleepy grin.

Sam yelled. "Looks like you're busted, Jason. It's Vice calling to check out this wild party of yours."

Harris responded. "I'm off of pizza duty so help yourself, guys." He moved toward the phone making signals to lower the volume of the radio.

He glared at Michael until he turned it down a little then he spoke. "Hello."

"Hi, it's just me."

"You're certainly up late this evening."

"Well, *The Late Show* just ended and I wanted to check with you before I crawled into bed."

"I'm glad you did. How's Joanna's leg?"

"She's taken a few pain pills, but otherwise she's feeling fine. How's things going there?"

"You can probably hear the guys are happy and getting rowdy as usual. We played cards most of the evening. We're dealing with the late-night munchies now."

"I know how that is. Did you win all of their money this time?" She asked.

Harris paused, thinking about his failed meeting and the expectations of landing that extra job and an envelope of money from Baldevino each month. His anger rose. He and the guys would be talking about how to get some payback from him later.

Pamela responded to his silence.

"Honey, are those guys distracting you again?" She smiled at how he had explained his silence in the past, not knowing that it was a lie.

"Yeah, and I'm feeling tired. You know how hard it is to get these guys out at a decent hour." He yawned to help persuade her that this lie was also the truth.

"Yes, and it's about time for me to get to sleep, too. You won't stay up all night, will you, dear?"

"I won't."

"Is that a promise?" She asked.
He grimaced and shook his head as he spoke. "Yes."

Chapter Twenty

"I don't think it was smart letting those two officers live." Jerry commented hoping to sound noncritical.

"I'm in this caper only to get those who tried to kill us. If they had resisted in the slightest I would have done them on the spot, too." Doug responded defiantly.

"I know how you feel about this, but papa has always told me that leaving too many loose ends usually brings us a lot of grief later."

"Maybe, but a death sentence that's carried out so casually as that is just not right."

"That shouldn't matter too much when you need to protect your future. If one of those men whose life you spared tonight decides later to get brave and then manages to identify you, leaving the country may not be enough to keep you safe or out of jail."

"Until that actually happens I'll continue thinking that

I'm right about that sort of thing."

The van turned onto Harris' street.

Doug's mind raced to scan and commit to memory the details of the area. Scattered trees lined the block with at least one in front of each home. The streetlights were well placed and easily lit most of the sidewalks. A number of cars were still parked on the street.

Most porches were dark. Lawn sprinklers had been activated in front of one home.

Jerry pointed at Harris' house as they passed it.

Doug was able to only look briefly. They parked down the block between two autos that were partially shaded from a nearby streetlight. Harris's house was across the street and on the other end of the block.

Doug shifted slightly in his seat and pulled the black bag from the seat behind him. He rummaged for a couple of seconds and located the silencer for his .45 caliber semi-automatic pistol.

Jerry watched for a moment, then slowly a smile covered his face. "You sure look comfortable doing that, pal. I'll bet this is not your first time on a hit."

Jerry chuckled.

Doug's smile dripped with sarcasm. "Don't get any ideas that we'll be setting up a shop together."

Jerry's smile widened into a grin, as Doug finished assembling the pieces of hardware.

Jerry needled him about being a hitman. "I was thinking there might be a huge demand for the highly selective type of work you do."

"Well don't! When Harris is dead I'm retired."

"Could be some really big money." He joked.

Briefly Doug stared unforgivingly at him then continued to resolve several more items on his mental checklist. He donned a dark jacket and gloves, slid the pistol into his waistband and was ready to go.

"I'll do a quick reconnaissance of the grounds and be back in twenty minutes. If there are any problems on the street, sound one long blast on the horn and then get the hell out of here as fast as you can."

Jerry nodded.

Doug moved to the second seat and opened the sliding door. Instantly the courtesy light blared at him in the darkness. He reached for it.

Jerry's hand reached and interrupted him.

"I'll take care of that. You get out of here and don't forget to be careful."

Doug exited and silently closed the door.

He noticed the lingering smell of pine. He sighed for the old days associated with that smell.

He paused and listened.

The neighborhood was strangely silent. Briefly his ears sought aural sensation. Where were those *all to common* noises—the faint hum of a hissing power transformer, the low clatter of a neighbors window air-conditioning unit, the feline courtship ritual from a nearby back yard?

Was the neighborhood holding its breath as if to anticipate what might occur over the next few hours?

Doug released those budding thoughts.

This was the time for images of strength, revenge and death. Not pretty sights, but they are very necessary ones when society neglects to properly tend the primal needs of its people.

When power is abused, it must be surrendered. When-
ever that fails, death is one of the remaining alternatives.

He crossed the street to the comfort of deeper shadows.
Harris' house was about a hundred feet away.

A light breeze rustled overhead leaves.

He avoided walking on a wet sidewalk and the telltale
tracks that it would produce. Finally he could clearly see
the illuminated windows of the house.

He strolled out of the shadows and into the pale illumi-
nation produced by a streetlight.

The lawn seemed recently cut. Two late model cars sat
in the driveway and one on the street. It was a nice neighborhood and a nice house.

Boldly Doug strolled up the driveway along the shad-
owy side of the vehicles. He turned toward a side door and
heard a burst of men's laughter.

Through partially closed slits in the mini blinds he saw
their shapes. A half-open window emitted food smells.

He walked between the house and the garage.

Turning the corner he took off a glove and stooped to
touch the grass. It was dry. He pushed a finger into the
soil. It was also dry and firm.

He replaced the glove and smiled. There would be no
tracks left here either.

His first need was adequate concealment if it were to
become necessary. Cautiously he walked the boundaries of
the backyard. The clump of bushes in one corner would do
fine, he thought. He inched sideways into them and squat-
ted for a moment to check them out. *Excellent. Observing
the back of the house from here would be quite easy.*

Next he moved along the back edges of the house inspecting each window that had an open shade or curtain. All afforded partial views into some other portion of the home. He walked along the side of the house, stopping at a living room window to observe.

A six-foot fence covered his back.

He inspected the room. Hardwood floors held sturdy furniture. Occasional area rugs dotted shiny waxed wood. Browns and blues mixed throughout the color scheme. The room was neat and orderly. Indirect lighting along an interior wall bathed the room in a soft glow that produced a subtle mix of light and shadow.

The latest popular music played much too loud for two o'clock in the morning. Beside the front door was a three-legged entry table, holding four holstered pistols and a large pile of car keys.

Another round of laughter thundered through the rooms. Unable to hear the joke Doug smiled knowing it was related to one of three topics, the favorites of most men—bathroom functions, sexual body parts or racial and ethnic put-downs.

Moving again to the backyard, Doug stopped outside the entrance of the laundry room. From there he could see directly through it and into the kitchen.

Four men sat in a cluster, mostly eating and occasionally drinking. Clearly it was a gathering of men comfortable around each other.

Another round of laughter broke the night's silence.

📖

Earlier Jerry had watched as Doug left the van and

moved stealthily toward Harris' house. At the last minute before Doug disappeared into the backyard, he adjusted his side mirror to better view the area.

That was ten minutes ago.

Now he wondered what was happening.

Would all hell suddenly break loose or would Doug be able to finish his business in a quieter way?

With others in the house he hoped that nothing would be happening any time soon. Hopefully Doug was smart enough to wait until they were gone, he thought.

Jerry remembered the meeting from earlier in the year. It occurred a few weeks after Doug and Kely had returned from their Caribbean cruise.

His wounds from the shoot-out at Mr. C's Brentwood estate had mostly healed. Jerry was determined to properly thank the man who had saved his life. Doug seemed highly embarrassed by the display of thanks he offered at *The Sandalwood Café and Restaurant*.

The entire lower deck had been rented in Doug's honor. A photo of his face was enlarged and stood ten feet tall against one wall. A rock band had been hired to play all his favorite music. Finally Jerry made a long mushy speech designed to praise someone who would rather have had none at all.

Halfway through the evening he approached Doug sitting at a table near the door.

"Forgive me, if this is a little too much. You look like you're overwhelmed by everything. I'm really thankful for what you did for me."

He held out a strong hand.

They shook firmly and Jerry sat in the next seat.

For the next couple of minutes there was silence. Each had taken several sips of their bottled beer before either of them dared to speak.

Doug commented. "I saw that *eagle, globe and anchor* tattooed on your shoulder."

He responded. "Oh, was that why you helped me?"

"Yes." Both men stared at a young couple dancing.

"Do you happen to have one, too?" He asked.

"Yes."

Jerry turned to look at him. "I should have known. What else would have caused a man on your particular mission to stop what he was doing and aid the enemy?"

"That's how *The Corps* trained us." Doug quipped.

"Yep, but I'm less motivated by it than you seem to be." Jerry responded.

The rest of the evening was more of the same kind of dialogue—the male banter and ritual of getting acquainted with another man.

It brought a smile to his face.

Their common history with the Marine Corps had given them a strong bond. Their mutual likes and dislikes formed another strong link for them to share.

Later that same evening, Doug introduced Jerry to Kely for the first time.

📖

Doug moved to the side window so he could hear more of their conversation. Although exposed from the street he decided to take the risk.

He leaned on the edge of the door.

"There was a Catholic, a Jew and an Atheist on an airplane." Barney began.

An uproar of complaints filled the room and Sam's voice rumbled it. "That's enough, Barney, sounds like you have had enough and it's gone right to your sense of humor. Somebody grab that man's glass before he gets any drunker or makes any more jokes."

Playfully Michael reached for it.

Barney handed it to him and grabbed for the bottle. Leaning back in his seat he turned up the bottle and guzzled three long swallows.

He slammed it onto the table. Harris glared at him for nearly making a mess. Their eyes met.

Barney held up his hands as if to surrender.

His mood changed a little. Rum trickled down his chin and onto his shirt. "That won't stop me, but I suppose the jokes are getting pretty lame."

Sam nodded.

Harris added. "I'm beginning to feel it, too, guys." He yawned wide so that all could see him.

"Come on, Jason. I've seen you be the last man standing more than once." Barney added.

"Well, not this time." He yawned again to emphasize his growing weariness.

Looking quite sober Barney quietly asked. "Do you have any idea what actually happened at the warehouse tonight?"

"I've been thinking about that for a while now and all I

can figure is that one of those fucking dirtbags managed to live through it all. Nothing much else makes any sense."

Sam nodded again. He did not normally drink this much and it had made him quite sleepy.

"What's your best guess?"

Harris began his supposition. "I think that piece of shit Carlson is the best choice for surviving it and then doing something like this. I learned last year that that fucker doesn't know when to leave things alone."

Disagreeing, Barney shook his head. "Well, what do you think about that faggot kid of Bruno's?"

Harris laughed. "That limp-dick rich kid couldn't get an operation like this started on one of his best days, much less contribute anything significant to it. How that Mafia punk ever got through the challenges of marine bootcamp and then into *The Corps* I'll never know."

With a jerk Barney saluted him. "Semper Fi, Lieutenant Harris." He laughed and Sam joined him.

"Cut the shit, you morons. This is serious, okay?"

Barney regained his composure and asked again.

"So you think Carlson's the likely one. Could he have sliced those guys up like that?"

"Probably, but I don't really think it was him. There was way too much blood around him the other night. He had to be hurting pretty badly. If he is alive, he's got to still be in very bad shape."

"Are you going to finish the job if he's still alive."

"Probably." Harris looked at his watch. "It's after two, fellows. I'm fading fast."

This time the men took his hint and after hasty goodbyes were gone within three minutes.

Harris went to a cabinet in the dining room to get his best sipping whisky. Immediately he took two big swigs and walked to his favorite chair.

Tottering for a moment he collapsed with a thud into the chair. The bottle was titled in his lap.

Yawns came to him quickly now.

His head began to spin.

To stop it he tipped the bottle again and took two more long swigs. Clumsily he guided the bottle to a coffee table, but failed to notice the small picture of Pam and him that he accidentally knocked to the floor.

With open eyes his dreams arrived.

Chapter Twenty-one

Only minutes before Jerry watched as Doug stealthed back to the van. He smiled at the antics, but recognized the necessity and that Doug was much better at it than he was.

As Doug slid through the door, he was ready for war.

"Quick, get that Uzi in my bag. We're going back and shoot every one of those fucking douche bags, right now. I've had enough of their scheming and underhanded bullshit. It's time for us to act and rid the world of that *holier than thou* trash."

"Hold on, pal. What's got you so riled up?"

"Those fuckers are talking about finishing the job on us and I don't want anybody left alive who even discusses those kinds of ideas."

Doug had already extracted another .45 from his bag and a hand full of extra clips.

"Hold on, Doug. We can't do that, not just now. That

kind of a shoot-out will bring enough cops here to hold a policeman's benefit. Get a grip on what you're saying. It's just plain stupid, buddy. This situation is not much different from any of your patrols back in *The Nam*. Remember for a moment what you had to do then. If you weren't in control, then your enemy was and if that was the case, you know you would have come home in a body bag."

"Well, I'll need these extras just in case."

Jerry laughed and grabbed Doug's shoulder guiding him firmly into the front seat. "Come on, Doug, my friend. Unless we blow it, there'll be only one shot fired here tonight. That's it."

Doug took a deep breath before he responded.

"Some of those law and order cops are such low-down conniving snakes. I can actually feel my own skin crawl and my temperature rise just thinking about their low-life tactics and their bragging bullshit."

"That's a big problem, pal, but not one for us to be doing anything about tonight. With his friends now leaving you can march right in there and do your job, right?"

Doug watched Harris' friends drive away. He grew calmer and then spoke. "I think so. Let me go check."

Jerry stopped him. "Wait a minute. First, let's make sure we've got everything in order."

Doug paused to listen.

"One shot, right?" Jerry reminded him.

Doug nodded and sighed.

"Make it an accident if you can." Jerry smiled.

He responded as if he were calm. "Got it."

Next, he slid from the van and made his way to Harris' house. After briefly going behind the house he reappeared and signaled for Jerry to approach.

Jerry moved cautiously from the van and a few moments later stood next to Doug where he whispered angrily. "Why the hell do you need me here?"

Pointing through the window, Doug spoke softly. "Look at him in there, he's either asleep or passed out."

Jerry's eyes widened at the sight then he whispered. "How do we get in?"

"This door and the one in the back are locked. I'll check the one in the front now."

Doug strolled toward the street and into the front yard as if he lived there. The street light and porch light caused him to grimace, but he fought the feelings.

He took a deep breath and grasped the doorknob.

Slowly he turned it. It was unlocked.

He paused and placed his other hand on the grip of his .45. He withdrew the pistol so it would be ready to fire. He had already chambered a round. Now he clicked off the safety and slowly pushed the door open.

Anxiety filled him as he stood in the doorway with his .45 pointed directly at Harris' head.

He stepped forward. Harris did not move.

Doug silently closed the front door and locked it.

He went to the side door and opened it for Jerry.

"This is way too easy." Doug whispered.

Jerry shook his head at Doug's comment. "Does anything ever make you happy?"

"That's not what I meant."

Drawing his concealed .38 revolver Jerry walked to Harris' chair and nudged him with it.

There was no response. Doug moved behind him with

his pistol ready.

Jerry touched Harris' hand and whispered. "He's still warm, so I don't think he's dead yet."

He picked up Harris' hand a few inches and dropped it. It fell to the padded arm of the chair then over the edge and dangled several inches from the floor.

He looked at Doug. "How do you want to do this?"

"Wait a minute I'm not killing an unconscious man no matter what he's done to me or anyone else."

Jerry looked surprised. "Isn't that a bit of a chicken-shit distinction to make now?"

"Maybe, but I'm sticking with it. I refuse to kill anyone who's defenseless no matter what kind of a bastard he is. In *The Nam* I refused to do anything like that unless the other person was also able to do something to me. You can call it my own personal sense of fair play if you want, but no matter how much of a dumb-ass you think it makes me, I won't do it. That's exactly why I didn't kill those two cops earlier tonight at the warehouse"

"That's okay for you, but I'm sure as hell not waiting for him to wake up. That's just plain dumb."

Doug nodded and turned away for a moment.

"Look in that desk over there for his gun cleaning gear." Jerry said, pointing across the room.

Doug went to it and after moving several items aside, he carefully replaced them. In the bottom drawer he found an old shoebox with gun oil, brushes, a rod and a dozen remnants from an old military T-shirt.

This is a lot like how my gun cleaning gear looked the last time I saw it. He smiled at the assortment of items and moved the box to a table in front of Harris.

Jerry had been exploring another part of the house and returned with a 9-mm semiautomatic pistol that had been stored in a leather gun pouch.

He laid it on the table among the gun cleaning gear.

"What's next?" Doug queried.

"I just need to make a few adjustments here and it'll all be set. Why don't you head back to the van? I can handle the rest of it from here on in."

Doug looked surprised, but moved toward the door. He turned to look as Jerry continued with his plan.

From the porch he walked straight down the front sidewalk and into the street where he headed for the sidewalk on the other side.

Ten seconds later as he was walking toward the van, a single gunshot cracked in the night.

Epilogue

For Doug the return flight to Cabo San Lucas seemed much shorter than the first one. During the final minutes of boarding some of mama's friends rushed the plane hoping to be included on the flight.

The pilot took them all.

The two men slept much of the trip and found very little time to sip their usual brewsky's and trade untold Vietnam War stories.

An hour into the flight Doug built up the nerve to finally phone Sammy and propose to her. He fumbled his words a bit at first, but eventually got them all out.

Sammy accepted the proposal with tears in her eyes. All agreed that her stunned excitement rivaled Kely's of just a week earlier.

The excitement of another engagement around *The Desert Phoenix* did not subside until after their flight landed.

With Kely and Jerry's wedding planned for mid-April of 1991, they decided to set theirs in late June.

The entire clan met them at the airport accompanied by off-duty servants and their closer long-term neighbors. The fiesta continued for hours.

Maybe it was the *warm fall winds* around Cabo San Lucas that made neighbors friendlier or maybe it was a personal quality of those few who chose to tolerate the intense tropical conditions. It was an accepted fact that neighborly interactions seemed to be a bit more commonplace in this particular part of the world. Many watched it happen around them. None could fully explain why it occurred, but all liked it.

Since Bruno's death mama pledged that she would not ever return to the United States to live. Most thought it was because of papa being buried at *The Desert Phoenix*, but no one wanted to discuss it with her for fear that an unresolvable argument would result.

After the three tutors arrived for the girls, Julia finally confided to Kely that she did not mind the strong sense of isolation any longer and was ready to stay with mama until she died. She reasoned that being isolated in the Cabo estate was no different than being isolated in the one back in Beverly Hills.

The girls were happy to stay and spoke excitedly of *The Desert Phoenix* as being much more fun than living in the big house back in America.

For the next week Doug and Jerry became non-shaving laid-back beachcombers. Each wanted to relax from the Los Angeles affair, but they each chose to do it in very different ways.

Jerry awakened late in the morning and drank his first beer for breakfast. He lounged most of the day in the blistering sun, napped during the late afternoon and then partied and drank heavily until after midnight.

Usually Doug was up with the sun.

He jogged regularly on the beach and sunbathed only for an hour or so in the late morning. He took long walks on the beach with Sammy to plan their future and was often ready for bed by 9:30.

Sammy decided that it was time to put her long unused clothing design education into real practice. After a week of talking about it she called her pit boss in Las Vegas and diplomatically quit her dealer job.

Then she and Kely began making plans to open a boutique after they both had become married ladies during the next year. Sammy planned to do all of the designs and production. A week into the planning process Kely also called her boss and resigned from her job, so that she could run the retail portion of Sammy's budding enterprise.

After leaving Los Angeles Doug wondered several times if Agent Townsen's people had been able to penetrate the details surrounding the situation with Harris. He remembered Townsen's boasts last year that one of his agents had kept Doug under surveillance during the final battle with Mr. C.

While he praised them for their assistance back then he doubted if they had located many of the details about this confrontation. He wondered if Townsen was still attempting to make contact with him. Each time the thoughts arose, he smiled and let them go.

Doug and Jerry talked for most of the first week about

the future of the investing company. Doug's absence during much of the prior week was proof enough that it could operate and flourish without his full attention. With the ending divestiture of Bruno's share of the company business, the cash stream it relied on for funding the stock market machine would disappear, so plans needed to be made for their replacement.

Peter, Doug's assistant, was promoted to manage the daily trading and, of course, he was paid a much bigger percentage of the earnings.

Agreement was also reached that the new level of funding would be forty million dollars and that Doug would pay twenty-five percent of that amount for a return of twenty-five percent of the net revenues. They would each receive smaller weekly payouts in favor of a retained-earnings program that would maintain the necessary cash flow to sustain the business.

Two weeks after the first reports of the unfortunate suicide of Detective Harris, Mr. Baldevino telephoned Jerry from Los Angeles. At first the discussion focused only on how mama was doing and how the rest of the family was recovering from papa's untimely death.

Later Mrs. Baldevino spent several minutes talking with mama about her plans for returning to the United States. Mama was quite tactful and agreed only that she might return for a short visit during the coming year.

When the phones were returned to the men, the conversation turned to other matters of interest to them in the LA area, especially about the families.

Among other items Mr. Baldevino recounted news that a week earlier Cecil Marcello, his bodyguard and three of his men were flying to San Juan in Cecil's new jet for a skin-diving weekend. For unknown reasons something happened to the plane about a hundred miles out of Miami.

Subsequently the plane went down and seemed to be lost with no survivors. The Coast Guard had just completed its usual search operations and finally declared that all passengers were missing and presumed dead.

Has Doug been at war too long?

As the final installment of *The Dying Game Trilogy* unfolds, Doug Carlson makes a startling choice that fills him with impossible questions. Although he is tired of fighting and revolted by the events of the past year he becomes a professional killer, but not for the customary reasons.

What propelled this unusual man to choose such a path? Facing challenges that pale before the Mob's onslaught, Doug's resolve is strong, but his internal struggle seeks attention first.

Choosing To Kill breaks new ground as it explores the issue of selective murder to further social and political goals.

Look for the fabulous conclusion of this series in 1999.

Visit PCP's home page at http://www.pacificcoastpress.com/